Peril without Mercy

Book 2

of

Apocalypto

Aedan Sayla
(originally published under the pen name Frank Carlyle)

Origins of Love Company

Cover Artist: Aedan Sayla

Aedan's books are available at: Amazon.com – Apple Books - Smashwords – Barnes & Noble – Kobo – Google Play Books – ebooks.com

Goodreads Page: Aedan Sayla

Author's Website: www.origins-of-love.org

Aedan Sayla's Blog – Musings: https://origins-of-love.org/musings

Author Contact Info: author-aedan-sayla@proton.me

Peril without Mercy / Aedan Sayla

Aedan Sayla

The Book List
(List last edited - 1/13/2023)

The Warriors of Mora Series
Book 1: *Submission of a Lady*
Book 2: *Warrioress Taming*
Book 3: *A Claimed Queen*
Book 4: *Possessing all of a Lady, Coming Soon*
Book 5: *The Unexpected Pleasure of a Slave, Coming Soon*

Apocalypto Series
Book 1: *A Drive to be Remembered*
Book 2: *Peril without Mercy*
Book 3: *The Will to Thrive, Coming Soon*

The Agents Series
Book 1: *Agent in Training*
Book 2: *Finding an Agent, Coming Soon*

Escaping Babylon Series
Book 1: *Foreign Princess, Coming Soon*
Book 2: *Queen in Hiding, Coming Soon*

The Badlands Series
Book 1: *The Baron Killer, Coming Soon*
Book 2: *The Cold Killers, Coming Soon*

American Apocalypse Series
Book 1: *City - Prison Land, Coming Soon*
Book 2: *Forest - Freedom Land, Coming Soon*

Standalone Books

Book: *The Huntsman*
Book: *Man on Fire*
Book: *A Russian Rose*
Book: *Tomorrow's Woman*
Book: *A Lady's Worth*
Book: *Charity's Gunman*
Book: *A Rebel's Persuasion*
Book: *Book Mate*
Book: *Brides of War*
Book: *Broken but Undefeated*
Book: *Cave Man*
Book: *Surrender's Passion*
Book: *The Forbidden Zone*
Book: *The Slave Princess, Coming Soon*
Book: *Lost, Coming Soon*
Book: *The Last Incan, Coming Soon*
Book: *His - Beauty in the Dark, Coming Soon*

Content Warning

Dear reader, if per chance you did not see otherwise – this is a work of erotic fiction. The erotic content is quite vividly portrayed.

All primary sexual relations that take place are of a heterosexual standard and the age of the characters involved is 18+.

There are several scenes of apocalyptic violence. There are also scenes where a character has to deal with past sexual trauma.

The appropriate reading age is 18+.

"8 If thou know not, O thou fairest among women, go thy way forth by the footsteps of the flock, and feed thy kids beside the shepherds' tents.

9 I have compared thee, O my love, to a company of horses in Pharaoh's chariots.

10 Thy cheeks are comely with rows of jewels, thy neck with chains of gold.

11 We will make thee borders of gold with studs of silver.

12 While the king sitteth at his table, my spikenard sendeth forth the smell thereof.

13 A bundle of myrrh is my well-beloved unto me; he shall lie all night betwixt my breasts.

14 My beloved is unto me as a cluster of camphire in the vineyards of Engedi.

15 Behold, thou art fair, my love; behold, thou art fair; thou hast doves' eyes.

16 Behold, thou art fair, my beloved, yea, pleasant: also our bed is green."

Song of Solomon 1:8-16 KJV

CONTENTS

Gone Crazy

Would nothing ever be the same again?

The answer was - No!

Grimly, I glanced away from the mile-long line of people waiting for a handout of food from the FEMA wagons.

Once again I made myself the promise that I would not be one of those people.

I hurried on, but as usual, my appearance in town attracted notice, because I always brought food with me. Fresh food and not the pre-packaged salt bricks that FEMA passed out.

What the long-term effects of consuming such prepackaged food would be I did not want to speculate as to.

The desire for something better than it already had people clamoring about me offering anything and everything by means of payment for what I carried in the sack on my back, but shouldering past them, I stepped up the stairs of the town's surviving church that had been turned into an orphanage and made my way inside leaving them behind.

Once again, I was surrounded by a clamoring mob, but this time I didn't mind.

Pastor Joseph Orndorff glanced up from where he sat at a desk and gave me a broad smile and said by way of greeting, "Bless you, Adam! This is your second trip to town this week! Things going better with the plantings than you anticipated?"

"They are believe it or not. Must be your prayers doing it though." I responded back with as I passed off the heavy sack of food to him.

He took it and with his other hand, he squeezed my arm as saying in a softer tone of voice not meant for the kids to hear, "Thank you, Adam. You know how I hate to feed them that garbage from the wagons."

I ducked my head down and shrugged as I turned to view the room full of excited kids of varying ages ranging from toddler to preteen now filled with joy at the prospect of eating something good for dinner.

"Don't mention it." I said softly.

Pastor Joseph patted my back hard, "I will most definitely mention it before God tonight! You're a living angel, Adam!" He said, before moving off with the bag into the inner reaches of the church that nobody for the most part wished to attend anymore.

To a large degree within the minds of the community God had failed them and so they had moved on to make the best of what was the toughest of situations.

A poor choice in my opinion, as life without God, in my opinion really wasn't worth the living.

A few others felt that way, but that was it, just a few. The rest of the town of Transum, Oklahoma were out to survive the apocalypse of our time by any means at their disposal.

The fireballs that had destroyed life as we knew it had come just two years ago. The countryside had been decimated, with the cities a sheer disaster of unimaginable horror the likes of which kept one up at night and spurred the need to carry a gun. That is if guns were allowed.

Any gun seen was confiscated on the spot and its owner denied food rations for two weeks.

Needless to say every gun within the county had disappeared a long time ago into one of the white vans that made continuing circuits about the land doling out there prepackaged food meant to survive a millennia if need be.

No, life would never be the same. All there was to do now was to make the best of it and seeing that these children had something good to eat for the moment was my best attempt at doing so.

I cared far less for the adults, who roamed the town, as they had the ability to help out their situation, but none cared to try and so I'd given up on them. Growing your own food was by no means easy in the current climate let alone dealing with what the fat cat billionaires had done to the world in their gift of GMO products and population control chemtrail dusting.

What plants that had managed to survive through the dry conditions and fluctuating cooler temperatures didn't really stand a chance when it came down to trying to survive the soil itself.

The soil had been destroyed, at least the upper fertile layers of it had been.

In a combination of GMO enzymes released into the ground by GMO plants and ingredients within the heavy metal laden chemtrails doled out heavily just before the disaster two years ago the result achieved had been the rendering of the upper soil levels becoming inert of any nutritional or biological value.

The soil literally wouldn't grow anything or anything half decent anyway.

The only solution that I had found was to dig down and harvest soil not affected by the aerial sprays and use it for vegetable propagation. It was hard work and few wished to do it, especially as there was no gas to fuel the machines that could easily accomplish it.

The majority of people preferred to just rely on the white vans to feed them, as if they had become addicted somehow to the concept of not doing anything that would be too hard on themselves. The reality of it though was that they had seemed less and less human to me the longer time went on.

Even now they stared at me beadily from wherever they hung about the town, as if they were rats concocting a master plan of domination. I didn't care about being popular and I could take care of myself with or without a gun and yet the downward spiral I was witnessing in the majority of the populace left me wondering just where it would all end.

I struck out of town not bothering to take any of the wide open roads presented to me. I knew my way and without a qualm I stepped into the dry brush of the once fertile land that had become a wilderness of sparsely located weeds.

Weeds seemed to be the only thing flourishing these days as at least they had some tolerances to the chemicals used to render the soil's nutrients unavailable for normal plant growth.

My pace was quick as it was always a concern to me when I left my place unattended for any length of time. I doubted anyone in town despite the allure of food would ever care to make the five-mile hike, seven miles by road, journey to my place, but still there was the off chance that they would.

That was why I always varied up when I came to town so they could never build a routine of my movements by which to anticipate my actions.

Two years in the Marines had taught me to be cautious about ever establishing a pattern. As a former sniper, I well knew the benefit of keeping an erratic schedule.

Being a Marine was one thing in my life though that I'd like to escape from and I had tried. I'd come to this remote area and bought my farm and for five years things had been blissful and I had found a peace of sorts, but now...... now my new found dream had been taken from me by circumstance and a global conspiracy of epic proportions.

Now more than ever my particular skill set of once being a warrior seemed to come to the forefront. I hated it, but at least it served me some good.

Like right now!

I ducked and the arrow shot from a makeshift looking crossbow skipped on by me to slam into some brush. I rolled away athletically and sprang up to my feet to run a short distance before diving into more cover.

I kept moving and within seconds I was in a hidden, undisclosed position out of the direct gaze of where my hunters had been located.

Patiently, I waited.

Minutes stretched by and I felt the palm of my hand holding a five inch double bladed boot knife get sweaty. Then in the distance came a cranky sounding voice, "Oh come on Zeke. That wasn't no towel head anyways."

"So what. He might've had something on him that we could use for trade."

"The only trade item we need is some more towel heads. Now come on! I'm starting to not like the smell of these scalps so much. Besides that they're making me hungry."

Both men laughed together and I stole out of my position and crept to a ridge that gave me an overview of the two men walking away across the wilderness. They were scalp hunters, paid killers for the government, such as it was.

Their sole job was to travel through the outer areas and look for the fall guys that had been blamed for the decimation of the cities in the East. The rumor went that when the asteroids had wiped out the West Coast along with other parts of the world that Middle Eastern jihadists had seen their chance and had taken it in the societal upheaval that had followed the disaster.

They had set off dirty bombs all along the east coast and millions had died and millions more when one bomb had gone off as an EMP and taken down the electric grid for good. Ever since then every survivor of what was left of the country had taken it upon themselves to eradicate every last Muslim looking person that they came across as some sort of honor bound civic duty to those who had been lost.

The zeal was such in fact that one stood to gain profit by the killing of them and subsequently face scalping had become a highly profitable commodity if one could prove to the authorities that the face was Middle Eastern and hence likely Muslim.

How far America had fallen in but two short years.

Right now I'd rather be anywhere else in the world than this former entitlement society brought to grips with stark reality. Getting out of the country now though was a complete loss.

The East was unrecognizable and you'd grow a third ear before clearing the radiation along the coastline from all accounts.

This was assuming that all the reports one heard were true.

Who really knew for sure. As it was I knew of no one who had actually come from the East to verify all of the gossip of the FEMA personnel that had been passed along as if it was the gospel truth.

In general, I trusted FEMA as about as far as I would trust a snake with a sour disposition.

Once more, the urge to strike out and find something better than the decaying reality I faced daily, hit hard. The question remained though of who would feed the children in town?

My consciousness wouldn't condone the thought of having them turn into the bigoted zombies that the rest of the town seemed hellbent on becoming. The urge to go after the two men and kill them was overwhelming, but it would be murder, and above all else I wished to leave killing behind me.

I pulled back from view of them and headed back on my way to my homestead. About an hour later I saw the buzzards.

They of all the bird species seemed to be flourishing the most. I knew what their presence signaled and I wished to avoid the death I knew I would find beneath their drifting spirals, but my feet took me that way anyway.

Some things no matter how terrible, just had to be seen. It took me twenty minutes to come upon the four bodies in the sand.

Their faces were scalped clean away, but it was obvious by other visible trait markers to see that this family of four on the run had been of the locality of origin that had been branded with universal hatred by all remaining Americans for extermination.

Looking now though on the bodies left to rot faceless in the sun all I felt was shame.

What right did humanity have to exist when we perpetrated horrors like this upon each other?

Americans felt they were justified to murder an entire people group based on the hearsay of others as to what they had done, but the timed event of over twenty dirty bombs going off at the same time along the eastern seaboard was a hard nut to crack for anyone let alone terrorist cells hampered by a surveillance state the likes of which the NSA was capable of producing.

No, I tended to think otherwise, but I kept my objections to myself and unsaid, as the message of the day seemed to be one of hate.

People were out of love for one another and yet needing a powerful emotion by which to feed off of they had latched onto hate as something out of the ordinary and Muslims fit the bill nicely by which to enact it upon.

The hundreds of thousands of Middle Eastern refugees that had been imported just before the world chaos had ensued were meeting grisly fates like this every day.

There was little I could do for the bodies as I had no tools with me and the ground here was too hard to dig by hand.

Taking my hat off I said, "God, nobody deserves to die like this. I feel bad for these folks, but I guess what makes me feel bad the most is that, well, I guess, because I know they're not with You. That would make things better knowing if that was the case, but....... I pray that You'd have mercy on them anyway."

I put my hat back on my head and looked away as the bleakness of reality settled upon me hard once more. What was the purpose in trying to survive this apocalypse that had taken love out of the hearts of mankind?

"Where have all the good guys gone to, God?" I breathed out softly.

"I'm looking at one." Came the quiet response from within my soul.

Shaken, I looked about, but I knew. I knew who had spoken to me and knowing that I had God's attention caused me to fret as to what to do all the harder.

I couldn't bury the bodies, but I could do more than leave them like this.

Feeling the weight of a Divine gaze upon me I set about dragging the bodies closer together. That done, I went about prying up rocks and laying them gently over top of the bodies.

It was hard work in the afternoon heat, but I labored on until a solid layer of rock stood between the dead and the buzzards.

Satisfied, I nodded to myself and turned to leave this forlorn scene of death, which is when I saw her.

How I had missed noticing her up till now I did not know other than the fact that her clothing blended in like camouflage with the sparse weeds growing about her.

Her eyes were what attracted my attention the most though.

They were directed fully upon me and they were all I could see of her face, as a traditional hijab covered the rest of it along with her head.

She'd gone to some effort to conceal herself and it had worked, as she yet had her face and life to attest of, but she wasn't going anywhere.

As my eyes took her in I found the evidence of an arrow shaft pierced through the calf of one of her legs. Then, with a collapse of energy her head fell back to gaze up at the sky as she breathed heavily for a moment.

That arrow had been reused who knew how many times to take down fellow kinsmen of hers let alone others like me, who just happened to be moving through.

I had no doubts at all as to the internal infection the girl must now have raging within her.

What to do?

I couldn't take her with me being what she was.

It didn't sit right to leave her here suffering either though.

About the only thing that did make sense was to finish what had been started and end her life as mercifully as I could and then bury her with the others.

My stomach turned sour and twisted into knots as I stood gazing at her heavy breathing form.

She seemed to be unconscious. It would be easy to do.

I could snap her neck quick and clean and it would be done and over with.

Raising a hand to my sweaty brow I took in how bad it was shaking. I let it fall and glancing at her lying there helpless I turned away as I had no will within me to do what needed done.

I made one step forward toward my homestead and stopped. It was as if an unmovable wall constructed of my own consciousness stood barring my way forward.

I gazed skyward for a long moment. Nothing made sense anymore.

Turning my head, I glanced back to see her looking at me again. Nothing made sense, but being somebody else other than myself made the least amount of sense of all.

Turning, as I was galvanized into an action that would likely cost me my life, I went over to where she lay. She'd pulled debris over herself as best as she could and I had to admit to a certain degree of respect for her.

She was a fighter. She deserved a chance.

"God help me for no one else will!" I breathed out as I leaned downward to start tossing the rocks and debris that she'd covered herself up with away.

Her eyes were very feverish, but interestingly with closer inspection, they seemed more slanted as an Asian persons would be. She was breathing heavy and in her one hand she gripped a rock but it went unused.

I slipped my hands beneath her and cradling her gently I lifted her up out of the shallow depression that she lay in.

She was a slight little thing for sure, but the prospect of making it the remaining two miles or so to my place was not a light task with her now in my arms. Still, I owed it to her to try.

Her eyes stared at me and watched my every move and walking forward I heard the rock in her hand fall to the ground. Like it or not, right now I was her only chance and she knew it.

I cradled her to me ever mindful of the arrow through her leg, but still it was made abundantly clear to me the pain that she was in by the softly expressed cries that issued forth past her tight pressed lips beneath her veil.

It was torture to hear her pain and I thought about snapping her neck all over again.

It would be more merciful by far to do that, but those eyes!

The way they bore into me kept me pressing forward as quickly as I could go towards my homestead.

CHAPTER TWO

Promise Made

It was dark when Robbie's deep barks alerted me to the fact that at least all was well at my place. I got to the railing of the gate and Robbie jumped up putting his big paws on it as he sniffed at the unconscious woman in my arms.

"Come on get back!" I groused out, as I awkwardly unlatched and pushed at the gate at the same time.

Robbie got down and I slipped through the gate and re-latched it. With Robbie padding heavily along beside me I made for the house in the late evening gloom.

Robbie got to the door first and fastening his large mouth around the handle he twisted his head and the door popped open.

"Thanks, buddy." I said, as I moved into the dark house and made my way through it by memory.

Reaching my bedroom I laid her down on the bed. In the darkness I placed my hand to her chest to confirm that she was still breathing.

Awkwardly, I brushed my hand over one soft padded mound of a breast to rest my hand in between the shallow valley in between. She was breathing, but barely.

Rising up I fiddled in the darkness and soon had a candle going, which gave me the light I needed to fire up my oil lamp.

Its brighter glow lit the room up and I hung it overtop of the bed on a hook. I rarely used it, but this was certainly the occasion for it.

Glancing down I went still as my eyes took in her face that had become uncovered. Her features bespoke of a mixed parentage of Asian and something else most likely European in nature. She wasn't the typical Middle Eastern refugee that one ran across out here for sure.

All that dually noted what grabbed my attention the most was how utterly beautiful she was.

Pulling my gaze away from her face, I took in the arrow wound that was killing her. The arrow had passed cleanly through the lean muscle of the back of her calf and indeed as injuries went it wasn't life-threatening, but the infection from it was.

Angry red lines ran out from the wound up and down her leg. At this point saving her leg was doubtful, but I was going to try.

I pulled a bag out from beneath my bed. It was a grab bag that I kept there if ever I should need to leave the house in a hurry.

I accessed the medical side of it and pulled out a bottle of rubbing alcohol. I doused her leg wound thoroughly with it as well as the arrow shaft itself.

Pulling my knife out I cut the fletching off of the back of the arrow. That done, I stood up and fetched a hack saw I had in the other room.

Sweat rolling down my face I gripped a hold of the carbon arrow shaft and began sawing down at it from the backend in an attempt to split it into two pieces. Despite my hard stabilizing grip on the arrow shaft her leg was moving and glancing worriedly I checked to see if the pain from the motion had jarred her awake.

It hadn't and the fact that it hadn't drove me to work harder, as I felt sure she didn't have long. I pulled the hacksaw blade out and sawed down from the top briefly until a half section of the hollow shaft fell away with a clink to the floor.

I now had a channel about four inches long cut into the arrow. Going to the floor nearby I lifted out a board and reaching down my fingers claimed ahold of a shotgun shell.

Going to the bed, I used the hacksaw to cut away the wad and the buckshot until all I had left was the powder charge. Barely breathing as I focused tightly on my hand's action I sprinkled the black powder contents of the shell up-and-down the cut in groove in the arrow until it was full.

Reaching to the floor I picked up the lit candle sitting there. I gripped a hold of the barbed side of the arrow firmly and then for a moment paused.

Glancing up at her I said, "I'm sorry, but this is going to hurt - asleep or not."

Gritting my teeth I lowered the candle's flame to the powder and it flashed brightly even as I pulled the arrow clean on through her leg. The smell of burnt flesh had me wanting to throw up, but it was her scream of pain that unnerved me the most.

Throwing the arrow aside I hiked up further along the bed and did my best to comfort the suddenly very conscious patient I had just burnt with gunpowder from the inside out.

"Shhhhh!" I soothed, as I fought to hold her hands down and with her eyes blinking madly I watched her slip back under.

Fully subdued into unconsciousness again I let her hands go and turned back to her leg. It was bleeding openly in evidence that I hadn't cauterized the wound fully, which really hadn't been my intention anyway.

My goal had been to take out the heart of the infection and hopefully that at least had been done. Time would tell, though.

I let the wound bleed out some more before sprinkling an open bag of quick clot to both sides of her leg before I then wrapped it heavily with two bandages and a roll of gauze.

Her breathing was elevated and thready sounding.

Reaching into the bag on the floor once more I pulled out a syringe. It was a makeshift world we lived in now and this certainly was a make do remedy. It was a veterinarian cow antibiotic injection shot.

Rolling her sleeve up I sterilized an area of her arm and injected the needle into her smooth flesh. I knew full well that I could be killing her for good, if she was allergic to penicillin, as many people were these days.

Coming from a third world nation most likely, though it was doubtful that she was allergic to it, at least that's what I told myself. Whether the shot would do her any good was an even bigger question.

Pulling the spent syringe out I stared at her for a moment. The allure of her uncovered face sung out to me and now more than ever I really wished that she wouldn't die.

Closing my eyes, I stretched out my hand and laid it over her leg near her wound and said, "Please, God! Help her live. I don't know why, but I want her to live. I ask this in Jesus's, Name, even so let it be."

The prayer said I went about putting stuff away and then I covered her up with a blanket. That done, I went and got a drink of water and washed myself up.

Coming back to the room, I glanced at Robbie sprawled out on the floor beside the bed.

Glancing at her I asked, "Do you think she'll make it?"

His doleful expression wasn't hopeful and truly, that was how I felt too. I dimmed the lantern and taking one of the pillows off the bed I lay down beside Robbie, but sleep was far from me as I listened to the soft rasp of her labored breathing.

Closing my eyes I prayed some more. It was important that she live.

The why of that was something I didn't really want to investigate too far at the moment. She just needed to live.

Things would be better if she lived. Robbie seemed to think so too.

~~~~~~~~

Something was shaking.
~~~~~~~~

The bed was shaking!

Blinking away sleep I rose up off the floor to the sight of her convulsing upon the bed violently. For a moment I panicked about what to do before past training took over.

With convulsions there was little to be done, but there was one needful thing at least that should be done. I went around to the head of the bed and forcefully turned her head to the side, mindful to keep my fingers far away from her mouth.

She was already foaming at the mouth and then she was vomiting. My own stomach, dry heaved at the smell and the sound of her vomiting, but I steeled myself against being too affected.

It was hard not to be affected, though at the sight of her body flailing about upon the bed. It was actually dangerous to be near a person in convulsions as they possessed greater strength than typical and she was no exception to this.

I continued to keep my fingers away from her mouth and keep her head to the side so she wouldn't choke on vomit, until at last her body came to a rest.

All was not good though. She was literally burning up!

My hands came away from her head as if singed and I made the decision that her fever needed to be brought down. Normally not a good idea, as it was better to let a fever run its course, but her fever was simply too high.

I made a quick exit from the room as the morning sun rose up outside brightly.

Robbie looked on worriedly as I came back into the room with a basin of water and a rag.

I set the basin of water down and spared her a brief glance of apprehension before taking out my knife and cutting her clothes off of her until she lay there devoid of all covering.

Sweating profusely, I turned away and soaked a sheet in the basin of water before then dragging it across her naked form.

Her body turned the sheet hot and I took it off and re-soaked it and applied it again. I repeated the process several more times until something inside me said, "*Enough.*"

I pulled the wet sheet off her.

The bed was a mess and I hated to leave her in such a way, but to change the situation was to have to touch her.

It couldn't be helped.

I laid a blanket on the floor and then turned to her. Carefully, I slid my arm under the back of her thighs and my other hand beneath her upper back.

She was a slight little thing and I hardly had to exert myself at all to lift her up and transfer her to the floor. On inspiration I laid her onto her belly.

Closing my eyes, I forced myself to look away from the view of her perfectly shaped little rounded bottom and back to the soiled bed. I worked quickly and had it stripped and a new sheet on it within minutes.

Turning to her I got a rag and began to wash her back off.

Muttering under my breath I said, "God, I sure hope You know what You're doing, because I sure don't!"

Feeling intense guilt because of the visceralness of my desire for this poor sick woman I forced myself to continue washing her off as impersonally as I could.

Finishing, I dried her and once more lifted her to lay her back on the bed front side up. Continually grinding my teeth I completed the task of cleaning her up.

It had been a very long time since I had touched a woman and to do so now in such an impartial manner was literally torture.

She was beautiful and I wanted her.

Breathing evenly, she now rested peacefully upon the bed looking much better in color than she had earlier. She was going to live.

I covered her up with another sheet all the way to her chin. Her black hair lay strewn across the pillow beneath her head even as her exotically proportioned body was now hidden from view.

For the moment she was stable and backing away from her I took the opportunity presented and left the closed off atmosphere of the room. Breathing deeply I stepped outside into the morning sunshine.

The day was bright, but I felt like I deserved a lightning bolt.

My mind wouldn't stop!

Over and over my brain relived all that my eyes had taken in and that my hands had actually touched. To describe the condition of my manhood at the moment would be to say painful.

My pants simply weren't roomy enough to adequately fit how engorged I was with the desire for what I had seen and touched.

"God forgive me!" I groaned out, as I dug my hands into my eyeball sockets in an effort to erase a memory that was still replaying and imaginatively creating more at the same time.

The emotions of all that I wanted to do with her were so real that it scared me and whispering out loud, I said, "God, help me!"

"I am." Came an unexpected response in the midst of my angst over struggling to be a moral minded person versus the animalistic nature that had me aching to go back inside and use the girl for my own pleasure.

Then once more I felt the same voice that I clearly attributed to my Creator say, **"Enjoy her, son."**

"What?!" I breathed out in response, but no answer came.

"Enjoy her?!"

Still no response.

"She's a Muslim!" I exclaimed, but still no response came.

I couldn't marry a Muslim.

Somehow I must be deceived in this and yet just why did I want her to live so much, if there wasn't something I was wanting to occur between the two of us?

I didn't know. Out of the blue the planting beds came to mind along with their need for water.

I straightened away from the post and made to walk, but my shaft was a living agony within my pants. Breathing out resignedly I opened my pants and slid the zipper down.

Pushing my underpants down I bared my shaft to the morning sunlight. It really didn't take anything, but the lightest of touches and my shaft was instantly spasming as a sharp orgasm swept through me.

Closing my eyes, I let it sweep through me as jet after jet of semen shot out to soak the parched ground. Finally done, I closed my pants back up shakily and did my best to recover my composure from what undoubtedly had been the best and yet the oddest orgasm of my life.

As good as it had felt my sharpest regret was that it hadn't occurred while I had been buried deep inside of the object of my fantasies that lay asleep in the house behind me.

I started to go, but looking down at the seed soaked ground I heard the voice of my Creator once more say with an emphasis I couldn't deny, **"The next time will be inside of her. She is good ground."**

I closed my eyes for a moment completely humbled as what felt like a promise washed over me and which gave me some measure of peace that didn't make any sense.

"Why God?" I whispered out.

"It's not good for you to be alone. Now water your plants and when you return, she will be awake."

Obediently, I didn't question my Maker anymore, but I continued on to the garden patches. It was over two hours later when I stepped back within the confines of the house after having watered all of the plants successfully.

Quietly I made my way to the bedroom which wasn't very quiet with my boots still on as they were. I peered in and to my surprise I beheld Robbie sitting beside the bed with the most sublime of expressions on his face as a slim fingered hand massaged behind his ears repetitively.

The bum!

My eyes followed the hand up the arm to the white sheet that it disappeared under. From there my eyes met her engaging almond eyed gaze and I stood transfixed for a moment not knowing what to do.

Her gaze was many things: curious, watchful, unsure, but most notably of all lacking in fear. I saw no fear in her eyes for me and that was good.

Why was that good?

Shaking my head, I broke the trance she had me under and asked almost to myself, "I bet you're thirsty."

She did nothing, but stare inquisitively at me and with a bit of dread to my voice I said, "You don't speak English do you."

To this she nodded her head, '*no*'.

Sighing, I rubbed at my forehead and left the room to get her some water.

Her not knowing English was going to certainly complicate things. I got her water and reentering the bedroom I knelt down and held it steady for her as she weakly rose up to sip from the cup.

All the while as she drank one leanly muscled arm held the sheet tightly up around her neck and not for a moment did her eyes leave mine.

What did she see I wondered?

Breathing heavily, she lay back down. Glancing down I saw that the cup was empty.

This woman had some uncanny way of causing me to lose focus. I wasn't too sure I liked that about her.

She spoke in an Asian dialect and glancing at her I saw her motion to the glass. She wanted more.

"Uhhh no, honey. It's not good to get too much water too soon." I said, rubbing at my own stomach in an attempt to communicate that.

Amazingly, she nodded as if she understood.

Raising a hand slowly I watched her eyes track its progress until I laid it over the top of her forehead.

It was still hot, but nothing like before. I looked down at her leg and moving down that way along the bed, I started to raise the sheet slowly.

I glanced up at her to see how she was reacting, but her expression remained enigmatically hard to read. Bringing my eyes back to her leg I took in the bandaged area.

The bandage still looked good. I'd change it tonight.

Running my finger along her calf further up past the wound I looked, but I couldn't find the red lines that had been there earlier. That was very good to see, but I didn't want to rejoice too soon.

I pulled the sheet back down over her leg. I glanced up as she said something softly in her own language.

What she'd said was Greek to me, but somehow I knew that she was thanking me for what I had done to save her life.

"You're welcome." I said, just as softly as she had spoken.

Getting the glass I got up and left the room. I went about making some chicken broth from a few of the remaining seasoning packets I had and when it had cooled enough, I poured a glass full of it and went back into the bedroom.

She'd been asleep, but her eyes opened and there for just a moment I saw fear and her body gave a slight start before she recognized me.

I'd stopped when I saw her fear, but now I continued on to her.

With eagerness for what I held she hiked up in the bed and I gave her the glass to hold for herself. She took it and shakily began to sip the warm broth.

Not meaning to, but it being unavoidable to do so my eyes gazed down the graceful plane of her back that lay nakedly exposed to me. Feeling myself react to the sight of her bare skin I turned my eyes away to gaze at the floor.

Reaching across to a nearby table I picked up the spent syringe I had injected into her. Her eyes came to me and I gestured to her arm.

Absently one of her fingers felt over the spot I had injected her at and I said, "I need to get more of this, if possible." I waved the used syringe and pointed to it and then I pointed to the clock on the wall and held up as many fingers as I thought it would take me to get to town and back. I made enough gestures to illustrate fully that I would be leaving soon.

Her eyes lit up with alarm and she shook her head no in a sharp gesture that sent her coal black silk like hair cascading about her bare shoulders. The plea in her eyes for me not to go was sincere enough to read even though no words had been spoken.

She didn't want me to go.

My stomach feeling funny within me, I softly insisted, "I've got to. You need some more help to get through this safely."

To my shock then I saw a big tear fall out of the corner of one of her almond shaped eyes and the sight of it slew me.

I had to go though.

It was for her best and to that end, I pointed to Robbie and gestured to say that he would stay.

Then not believing such a thing of myself, I went to the false floorboard and removed it and came back to her with a small 40 caliber revolver.

I set the pistol down on the bed beside her and she raised shocked eyes from it to me.

"I'll be back. I promise." With that said I literally tore myself from the desire to stay in the room and keep having her watch me like she was right now.

In a way I'd never felt so needed in my life and with that newfound desire to receive more of the same I took off for town at a pace eating run

CHAPTER THREE

Boxed In

Breathing heavy I came up alongside of the back of the church. The door was locked as I had expected it would be.

I rapped on it lightly, not wanting to draw any unwanted attention. If I could avoid being seen by anyone in town all the better.

This third visit within a week might really arouse some suspicions and above all I didn't need anyone dropping by my house while the girl was there. It took a while, but eventually the door opened and Pastor Joseph wordlessly pulled me inside.

Closing the door he locked it and in a serious tone he asked, "What's up, Adam?"

I glanced at two nearby girls and said, "Somewhere more private maybe?"

Pastor nodded and led the way. Soon we were in his office and with the door closed, we both sat down.

"You look rough, Adam. It's like you haven't slept all night on top of walking all the way back to town again."

I nodded and meeting his gaze I told him what had happened. Of all the people left in my acquaintance he was the only one I absolutely trusted.

He listened, saying nothing and for a while quiet reigned within the office after I had finished talking.

Then, glancing at me he said thoughtfully, "You say she's Chinese looking?"

Shaking my head I said, "No, I mean, yes, I guess. Really, she looks more Indonesian than Chinese, but it's like Chinese to some degree with a little bit of European thrown in there in the shape of her nose and some of the proportions of her face."

Pastor nodded and then giving me a direct look he asked, "Is she pretty?"

The question had been unexpected and inadvertently I felt my face flush red as I relived the moments of imagery of my patient's naked form.

Husky voiced I said, "Yes."

He nodded and got up.

Going to the door, he said, "Come with me, Adam."

Feeling a bit unsure of what he was up to I followed along dutiful-ly. We came to an overlook of the area below that was filled with screaming children dodging around in an old-fashioned rendition of dodgeball within the church's sanctuary.

Not being able to stop myself I smiled at their antics that for a moment took me somewhere to a better time than the one we now fought to survive in. Pastor's voice startled me as he said, "Being of the Far Eastern build I suspect she's a bit slighter of stature. That teenage girl over by the church door, would she be approximately the right size as your lady?"

Giving the girl a thorough look I nodded, "Close. She's maybe a little taller and wider in the hips, but less pronounced so in the chest."

"Got it. Now go back and lie down for a bit and I'll get some stuff together for her."

I really didn't want to stay long, but I grudgingly had to admit I could use some rest. Going back to his office, I lay down on the couch and the peace of a righteous man's place that had experienced much prayer overwhelmed me and I was asleep within moments.

~~~~~~~~

"Adam. Time to go." Came a voice from nearby and startled I sat up with one hand reflexively going to my knife tucked away in a boot.

Pastor Joseph smiled appreciably at the action and recognizing him I sat up and put my feet on the floor as I did my best to rid myself of sleep.

"How long was I out?"

"Oh, just a little over an hour. Come now, we best be going on or I won't get back before morning."

Startled by his comment I took in the rough clothes that he had donned and asked with surprise, "You're coming along?"

"I am. I've been meaning to come out for some time. Things are getting worse here in town and if the day calls for it sometime I might need to evacuate the children someday and well yours is the only place that comes to mind."

Nodding seriously, I said, "You're welcome to come. I mean that."

"I know you do, Adam. You're a good man."

Feeling embarrassed I got up and quickly we both went downstairs and out the back door that I had come through earlier. A serious faced teenage girl closed and locked the door behind us.

I prayed for the children's safety in the absence of their protector and from the silently moving lips of my companion I surmised that he was doing much the same.

The journey went swiftly under the hot sun, with thankfully no unwanted occurrences to mar the journey as had occurred yesterday.

As we made our way through the wilderness I made sure to point out landmarks by which to go by and being ever the one to pay attention to detail Pastor notated them down on a scrap of paper. The more I thought about it the more sense it made to have the children at the homestead and I said as much to him.

He nodded, "The time is coming for that I fear, but not yet."
~~~~~~~~

His reasoning didn't make sense to me, but I left it unquestioned. Robbie came out barking and looking truly ferocious and some part of me relaxed at the sight of him and his familiar bark.

"Relax boy, he's a friend." I said.

Robbie sniffed suspiciously, but relented with his aggression to allow Pastor Joseph to accompany me across the yard and into the house. I went ahead of Pastor into the bedroom and it was a good thing because her hand touched the gun lying on the sheet at the sight of another man with me.

I was about to speak up and gesture for her to know that he was a friend, when with surprise, I heard the same foreign-language the girl spoke rattle fluently from off of my friend's lips. The girl visibly relaxed at whatever Pastor had said to her.

Pastor glanced to me and smiling, he said, "Perhaps you could give us some privacy."

"Yeah, sure." I said awkwardly, as I backed my way out of the room and closed the door.

Feeling lost I sat down at the kitchen table for a moment before it occurred to me how bad I stank of the smell of sweat.

I glanced at the closed door and listened to the quite rapid sound of foreign voices from within it for a moment. The conversation didn't show any signs of letting up and so I made off to get clean.

An hour later feeling much better and dressed in fresh clothes I reentered the kitchen. I'd even taken the time to shave.

The door was still closed and I debated about what to do. I went to the stove and went about reheating the leftover broth from this morning.

The door opened and I glanced up to see Pastor. He saw the broth in my hand and said, "Ahhh good! She's starving, take it into her and then come back out and we'll have a chat."

I glanced at him oddly, but did as ordered. Stepping into the room with the broth the girl's eyes were quick to rise to mine and hold me with their usual mesmerizing grip.

I handed the broth off to her awkwardly, her eyes seemed to gaze upon me with a heightened fervency that was greater than before. She thanked me again and I nodded as I made my way back out of the room.

Just what had they been talking about for over an hour?

Pastor gestured to the table he was sitting down at and dutifully I sat down.

Gazing at me speculatively, he asked, "What are you going to do, Adam?"

I glanced to the bedroom. Glancing back, I said, "I was hoping you could help me with that. Once she's better she'll be able to travel, but is there any way you can convince her not to wear that face covering of hers? She really doesn't look all that Middle Eastern at all being more Asian looking than anything. I think she could make it if she ditches the Muslim garb."

Pastor was shaking his head back and forth and was giving me a look that said I didn't get it.

"What?" I asked defensively, not caring for his way of looking at me at all.

"Adam, do you seriously think the best thing for that young woman in there is to be turned out onto the open road as soon as she can walk? Muslim or no Muslim a woman on her own like that doesn't stand a chance. Think of what you would be sentencing her to Adam!"

"Hey look here, Pastor, I did my part and risked my life to save her when nobody else would have, except for maybe you. What more do you want from me?"

"Well, for starters, you could marry her." Pastor said matter-of-factly without even blinking an eye.

I felt myself go hot all over and the urge to protest such a notion rose sharply within me, "But.......

"But what?" Pastor interjected with just as passionately as I was in the moment.

"She's a Muslim!"

"So?" Pastor responded back with evenly.

"Well, I thought you weren't supposed to be unequally yoked and whatnot with an unbeliever." I said floundering about for something to say.

"The Scripture does frown upon it, but in the end Scripture does make some provisions for it so I see nothing wrong with suggesting it to you. This is a very unique situation. If she walks out that door, she's dead, Adam, and you know it. Being an unbeliever as she is tell me what that means."

My mind went instantly to the faceless people I had buried yesterday.

"That's right, it's not a good outcome. Have you become so hard that you can't see to make the situation work out for someone else other than yourself?"

"That's hitting below the belt a bit, Pastor." I cautioned.

"I know that, but what is it going to take to open your eyes, Adam? Through that door lies a young lady whose life is in your hands. Now tell me why you went to the effort of saving her only to deliver her up to her execution tomorrow?"

I didn't have an answer for that and so I looked away and remained silent.

Mumbling, I said, "She's dead if they find out that she's here."

"Not necessarily." Pastor commented before adding, "It's clear that she's of Asian origin and her language only testifies of that. You're in a unique situation here that might just be able to pull off a homerun if an investigation were ever to be launched. You're a farmer and lots of farmers, some even in this area, in the past got mail order Asian brides, as women can be hard to come by who are willing to share a lonely existence out here apart from society's former allures. You don't volunteer any information about yourself and for all purposes no one would suspect a thing for you being the lone wolf that you are to have a mail-order bride."

He painted a convincing picture, but he was leaving something out.

"Even if I did marry her, she wouldn't marry me Pastor. I'm a Christian!"

Pastor sat back in his chair and said, "Actually, Adam she has agreed to do just that. Not only that, but she's agreed to give up practicing her Muslim faith as not to endanger you. I get the sense that she is already heavily in doubt when it comes to her faith that she was born into."

I swallowed figuratively, as I felt a noose tightening about my throat.

"You have a great opportunity here to witness your faith to her. As it is you've made quite the positive impression on her already."

"I have?" I asked doubtfully.

"You have. She saw you bury people not of your faith and then pray over them, even though doing either is enough to get one killed these days. Now is not the time to lose being a witness for a soul contemplating the way it should go in life. Matters of the spirit put aside there are other things to be considered."

Giving me a direct look then, he said, "She's quite pretty isn't she. High time you had some help around here, and if I may be so bold as to say, a bit of sexual release, too? You remind me of a powder keg, Adam. You keep getting twisted tighter and tighter and if you're not careful you might just blow up one day soon and as you're my friend I don't want that to happen. She needs to stay here, but again as your friend I can't let you stay together and potentially risk you to the temptation that she represents and thus make you sin against God, because that's how you would see any failure on your part in concern to her. No, you need to see the facts and the fact is I think she'll be good for you. How about it, Adam?"

I turned my gaze away to the floor for a long moment before nodding my head in defeat to what he had proposed.

Pastor stood up and putting a hand to my shoulder, he said, "You haven't made a mistake, Adam. I'm sure of it."

"That makes one of us anyway." I said morosely, as he headed off back to the bedroom.

A couple of minutes later to my surprise, he reappeared with her. I wasn't quite prepared for the sight of her in blue jeans and a tank top T-shirt.

His arm around her, supporting her he helped her sit down in his chair. Glancing at me he said, "Her name is JaLin. Now I think we had better get started with this."

Before I knew it, he was quoting marriage vows out by heart first for me in English and then in the dialect of her Asiatic language.

Before too long I realized with some astonishment that I was a married man.

"Well, that finishes it now. You can kiss after I'm gone. I really need to be headed back."

Numbly, I nodded and getting up I awkwardly made for the bedroom.

Coming back from it, I extended out the handgun that I had given to JaLin earlier to Pastor and said, "In case things should happen."

He nodded thoughtfully as he stowed it out of sight in a pocket and said in a way that had a deeper reflected meaning to it than just the surface context of the words, "Thank you, Adam."

Stepping forward, he patted me hard on the back and then he was out the door and headed for town as fast as his feet could carry him back to his chief most priority in life.

I admired him more than all other men I had ever encountered in life, but this time he had really handed me a situation.

Slowly, my eyes left him to come to rest upon my wife's gaze. There was no doubt about it, she was a beautiful woman and dressed as she was now in a raggy T-shirt and a pair of tight blue jeans there was little left to argue against in terms of the erotic allure that she possessed as uniquely her own.

Coming unglued I rubbed at my stomach and asked, "Hungry?"

She nodded in a way that said she was starving and it was a look that I would never deny anyone anything let alone my own wife. Turning I went to a cupboard and proceeded to pick out some of my carefully hoarded cans of food.

Feeding her full with something of quality was suddenly very important to me. I went about opening cans only to realize that I was half starved for food myself.

Truly though, I was far more hungry for her than for food and yet now she was mine. I could do anything I wanted with her and it would be all right.

Closing my eyes against the sudden upsurge of all the fantasies engendered by my mind in relation to her I whispered desperately, "God help me!"

"I already have."

There was just no denying the trap that had been sprung expertly upon me and I gave in and stopped resisting it on the spot.

Turning I pointed to the cans on the counter and tentatively she pointed to the can of peaches.

She had a sweet tooth it would seem. I delivered the can and a fork to her.

My hand was moving away when her slim but strong fingers curled around it briefly.

I glanced up and the look I saw in her eyes needed no explanation. She was grateful for everything.

Nodding my head I said, "My pleasure."

I turned away and back to the other cans as my heart beat a little funny in my chest.

I went about making the fire in the stove so I could warm up the chicken noodle soup for her, but all the time my mind dwelt upon that look she'd given me.

That look had promised everything and increasingly I realized when it came to her that I wanted everything.

CHAPTER FOUR

Horizon

The days passed by and I found a lot to be both enjoyed in them and frustrated by in them.

It was so good not to be alone. JaLin had somehow become a fixture of my life already and it certainly was a direct result of her efforts to do so.

She cooked for me. She mended my clothes.

The house was always clean and she even helped me with the garden plots.

I'd never met a harder working woman.

I respected her on an entirely new level other than just being a survivor.

Communication remained difficult, but we managed.

I did have a problem though.

The desire to have her was driving me crazy, but how did you tell someone who couldn't even understand your language that the time to take your clothes off had come?

I found myself reluctant to do so as sexual pleasure aside, I hadn't had such a companionable good time with someone since...... ever. I didn't want to ruin that.

I especially didn't want her smiles to go away, but the desire to thrust deeply inside her and be one with her remained as a steady ache that was never far from my ever waking moment and that haunted me every night in my dreams.

I just didn't know about how to go about getting what I wanted.

She was in many ways still a stranger and yet I trusted her implicitly. I looked up from the Bible passage I had been reading and saw her gazing at me from the kitchen.

She smiled at me and feeling irresistibly drawn I got up out of the chair and laid the Bible down. I gazed at it for a moment and then at her.

She'd gone back to washing dishes and slowly I approached her with intent. I'd waited long enough and yet I still didn't want to scare her.

I made enough noise to let her know I was coming. I stopped just behind her so close that we were almost touching.

Her hands had stilled in the water and with commitment to the moment I slid my hands down her sides to settle them about her tiny waist.

She was a little thing, but beautiful in her proportions. Oh, so very beautiful!

I ached for her and to that end I pulled her back to me, enough so she could feel just how much I wanted her. There was nothing stopping me from everything I wanted, but I wanted input from her.

Leaning down I pressed my face into the side of her neck and kissed her where her neck and shoulder met. I felt her shiver appreciably when I did that and the desire to have her doubled.

I'd been no saint in my earlier life, but since becoming a Christian six years ago I'd not had a woman and now the desire to have this woman, who was mine threatened to overwhelm me with the intense desire of it.

Fighting hard to maintain order I focused on breathing evenly.

Gently guiding her to move off to the side a little I then lifted her up and turned her to sit on the countertop to the side of the sink. Her legs went to either side of me as I stepped in close.

I wanted her, but I wanted a consensus and not just a dictatorship on my part, at least this first time. She was breathing heavy and her face reflected nervousness for what was going down.

Sitting on the countertop she was at an even height for me now. Her eyes were on me and raising my hands I framed her oriental face gently and held it poised for my kiss.

Her plush lips gave way innocently against mine and I belligerently swept my tongue into her warm mouth. I was losing control and as the sweet taste of her mouth registered to me I lost it completely.

I held her head still for my domineering invasion of her. I'd meant to be gentle, but instead I felt overcome by the need she inspired in me.

Fighting hard I pulled back a little. It took everything I had though.

She tasted like heaven.

Tentatively at first and then resolutely I felt her hands slide around my back and then up to my shoulders. She in no way pushed away from me, instead her touch was a shy caress.

I pulled back, breathing heavy. She was too and then incredibly she smiled.

My shaft swelled even harder to be free of my pants and the strength of my desire for her was apparent. She glanced away from my pants with a blush to then tuck a strand of black ebony hair behind one of her perfect ears.

I didn't know where to go from here other than that we both needed a lot less clothing and that I needed to be in her. My eyes scanned down her torso to land upon her surprisingly curvy hips, only to lock upon the crotch of her jeans.

She'd been so embarrassed to wear these jeans at first and I'd rather gotten the impression that she'd never not worn a skirt in her life before. That said the imagery of her in these tight jeans had been one of the things persistently driving me nuts!

With my fingers shaking, I reached out and fumbling with the button loop.

I soon had it undone and the jeans unzipped. I glanced up at her as I began pulling them off her.

She hung onto the counter as the tight jeans slid free of her legs. Her eyes were bright, but not with fear.

She said something softly and a tremulous smile came out before she leaned forward and gave me a quick kiss on the lips.

That was all I needed and smiling I lifted her. With a little squeal she reacted a bit startled as I slid her down so her back was on the counter along with her head.

I held her gracefully formed legs up in the air against my one shoulder even as with my other hand, I grabbed a hold of her panties and forced them up and off of her legs.

I forsook my view of her face as I let myself revel in the view of my wife's most private area as I coasted my hands down her legs until pressing on the back of her thighs I spread her legs wide apart.

Her legs were somewhat resisting of the full exposure of her that I was engineering, but I easily overcame her resistance and then with hunger as I held her down with my big hands at the back of her knees, I lowered my head and licked my tongue up the full length of her very sweet, but tight looking sheath.

She was wet for me already and I feasted on her musky scent by spearing my tongue deeply into the wet slit of her womanhood.

She squirmed beneath me, but I went about tasting her all the more as I licked and kissed my way around my playground of newfound delight.

She bucked beneath me as I wetly kissed the swollen bud of her clitoris forward of her sheath and then she cried out with a moaned wail as I began to forcefully manipulate her center of pleasure with my warm tongue.

Her fingers speared into my hair, even though I knew I was probably giving her too much stimulation as to be almost painful and yet her hands did nothing to stop me and her open submission to me inflamed me all the more.

I channeled my approach to bring her pleasure and so I continued by indirectly moving my tongue about her pleasure bud, only to continually bring it back with rhythmic force directly focused upon it. She screamed, clutching hard at my head, but I didn't stop and soon she came again.

I wasn't satisfied though. Removing one of my hands from clasping the back of her thigh I poised my finger at her wet sheath and slid it in as far as it would go.

She bucked hard against my finger and I about came in my pants as she let loose with another orgasmic scream. She was so unbelievably tight about my finger!

Despite the passion of the moment and my almost being overcome I registered the fact of just how tight she was around a single finger of mine.

I'd heard that oriental women were smaller, but now I had the proof of it.

I ached all the more to experience the squeezing clasp I felt clamped all about my finger carried out all along my shaft, but just as surely I knew that while taking her would bring me pleasure it would also likely bring her pain.

I didn't want that, but I couldn't stop now.

Pulling my finger free of her with a sucking sound that made me groan I lifted her to be pressed down over the top of my shoulder. Her warm thigh right next to my face was irresistible and I kissed it as I turned to head for the bedroom.

She was mine. Mine!

Lifting my free hand, I placed it over top of the halves of her bottom in a possessive fashion as the full reality of how much fun it was going to be to have her around from this day forward occurred to me in fast-forward relief.

She hung over my shoulder unresisting and when I reached the bed I laid her down on it.

She wasn't a virgin, but I had expected that. The question remained though had she'd been raped?

My shirt already gone from me my hands went to undoing my pants that were about to burst apart at the seems, but all the while my eyes took in the fact of her closing her eyes and the action of her splayed apart legs closing quickly together.

Grimly, I reflected on the truth that she had a bad story of her own to deal with and right now I wasn't helping it. I couldn't help it though.

Reaching down I had to forcefully pull her thighs apart. That accomplished I got one knee in and then I was on the bed between her thighs, but she was a different person.

She was as stiff as a board and her eyes were so tightly shut that I feared she'd bruise her face. I glanced down and the imagery of my huge cock at the ready to plunge into the tightness that she was almost made me do so on the spot.

I so badly wanted to feel just how tight she was and make her stretch to fit all of me, but with a groan I admitted that I simply couldn't do it.

I let my head fall to rest on the pillow to the side of her head as I held myself still above her.

Her slim thighs were shaking to either side of mine and opening my eyes and turning my head I witnessed the imagery of tears bubbling up from her closed eyelids to spill down the sides of her face.

I just couldn't do it.

Feeling like all the life had been punched out of me I fell away from her to lay on the bed beside her. You would think that would've made her feel better, but she broke forth then with the most forlorn cry that I'd ever heard and the sound of it tore me to shreds.

More cries and wails bubbled up past her lips and then she was turning onto her side away from me and curling up in a little ball.

"Hey now...... none of that. I know... I......" I sighed out at a complete lack for words to comfort her as I forcefully turned her to me and brought her over to lay against my chest.

She didn't resist me, but instead she seemed to cry all the harder. I rubbed up and down her back as my cock in the aftermath of this bitter expressed outpouring of emotion receded once more to a semi flaccid state.

I was set to experience about the worst case of blue balls in my life, but strangely I didn't really care.

~~~~~~~~

Gently I eased her away enough so that I could get up off the bed. She'd fallen asleep hours ago and in a dilemma of not wanting to wake her I had just lain there with my cock repeatedly getting hard and soft and back again.

I knelt down beside the bed and whispered, "God please help her and me for that matter. I want to care for her right. Please help me do that!"

I looked up and my eyes took in the full curves of her bottom completely bare to my gaze as she lay on her stomach sleeping peacefully.

Closing my eyes as my cock and sore balls once more sprang to life I stated with meaning, "Please!"

I got up and walked stiffly away and out of the room. I needed a release bad, but I had a promise from God and so like it or not there would be no release, until it could occur in her and right now I didn't know when that would be.

My mind filled with the thoughts of the tension filled future ahead of me completely missed seeing her open her eyes to watch me leave the room.

I also missed seeing her pounding an angry fist over and over again into her pillow.
~~~~~~~~

~~~~~~~~

I slept on the couch the rest of the night and in the morning I slipped out of the house before it was time for me to customarily do so. In a way I was running.

I was running from the confrontation of what life would be like having to deal with what I wanted, but couldn't have, unless it came at the cost of her emotions and I didn't want to do that.

It wasn't right of me at all, but in a way I was angry with her.

It really wasn't a justifiable anger, but it was within me just the same. Knowing how unjustified my anger was towards her I also knew that she didn't deserve to experience it so the best thing I could do right now was to stay away.

The reality of it though was that I had to go back sometime.

In the meantime though I took out my frustrations by throwing shovelful after shovelful of dirt into the wheelbarrow that I had stationed close by.

The underlying soil layers unaffected by the soil modification chemical sprays weren't overly rich with nutrients fit to sustain plant growth except for here where I was digging.

I was digging into a topsoil drift that was a holdover from the dustbowl era of the early 1900s.

Top soil drifts like this were a great aid in speeding up the construction of new elevated planting beds to grow even more produce off of. That said, it was still tediously hard work, but today I threw myself into it with a gusto.

I don't know how many wheelbarrows I'd hauled and dumped when suddenly looking up out of the pit I beheld her standing there not too far off.

She held a basket in her hand and glancing at the sun I realized it was past midday already. Covered in sweat and dirt I looked around a bit sheepishly and blinked as I took in the amount of relocated dirt situated off where my new garden plot was going to be.
~~~~~~~~

I'd lost it mentally a bit today and suddenly I felt the effects gained from working like a madman for hours on end. She'd come closer and now silently stood at the edge of the pit that I was in.

She lifted the basket slightly and I looked away. I stared at my shovel handle for a moment.

I just couldn't be angry at her.

In fact, I had no desire to be angry with her. The situation was just outside easily dealt with parameters.

I laid the shovel side and climbed up my wheelbarrow ramp to where she stood. She surprised me then by taking my hand and leading me toward a promontory overlook not far away.

I went willingly and allowed my dirt encrusted hand to rest within the grasp of her small hand. Only now did the impact of blisters formed beneath my already tough calluses make a dent into my consciousness.

I'd overdone it a bit today. Worse than that is that I'd been too preoccupied in my wrath to be properly aware of my surroundings.

That was a dangerous thing to get slack about doing and I now scanned about looking closely, but all was clear within the wastelands that stretched out around us.

Reaching a good spot we sat down and she laid out a very thoughtfully arrayed amount of food in front of me.

She always did her best to please me with what food we had to work with, but she'd pulled out all the stops today. She was trying to say sorry to me in a way that I would understand.

I looked up from the food and read the confirmation of it in her expressive eyes.

"It's alright, JaLin. I'm not a……. I don't want to hurt you." In this moment I truly hated my lack of knowing her language, but she nodded her head and then reaching forward, she touched my hand and said almost unintelligibly in English something to the effect of, "I know."

Her attempt to speak in my native language instantly endeared the moment to me and I went about gladly consuming the food that she had brought.

I noticed that she didn't eat much of her own food, but that was somewhat typical of her.

I usually got onto her about it, but not today. Feeling full and very much of the opinion that I'd done enough work for one day I sat back intent to enjoy the day that had gotten a lot brighter somehow.

JaLin still seemed tense to me though, and pondering on that I watched her as she studied the picturesque view that the elevated knoll afforded us.

She glanced my way questioningly of my stare upon her and I gestured to the horizon and asked, "You like the view?"

She nodded, smiling and said a word that I had come to attribute with meaning '*yes*'. Then she gestured to me in the way I had to the horizon and the way she did it made me conscious of the fact that she was saying she liked me far better than the horizon.

My mouth dry I watched her get up. She'd worn a skirt today and idly I recognized it as having once been a house curtain from upstairs.

She was very adept at sewing to be sure and somehow she'd made an old curtain look quite becoming as a dress.

She came over to me and knelt down on her knees. Her breathing was thready but with determination, she leaned forward and kissed me.

It was a passionate kiss and as always I reacted to her, but I made no move to touch her. She pulled back and gazing at me enigmatically for a moment she then made a come-hither motion with her finger and got up.

She turned and walked forward towards her pretty horizon without another word.

Feeling drawn by her I got up and followed along slowly behind her. She stopped after a little ways and set a small bottle down upon a rock and then moved on forward several more paces to where a log lay forlornly alone all by itself.

I reached the location of the bottle and stooping down I picked it up. It had a small amount of what I took to be olive oil in it.

Glancing towards her in puzzlement I beheld with shock as she knelt down before the log and with both hands reached back to pull her skirt up to pile up on her back as she bent over before the log. My shocked gaze instantly took in the fact that she wasn't wearing any panties!

Instead of gazing at the ground before the log though she placed her head on her hands that gripped the log as she continued to stare at the horizon that both she and I found beautiful.

Her posture was such though that she had arched her back deeply down and even now was erotically offering me the view of her backside and the spread apart lips of her womanhood in as clear of a sign of an erotic offer to a lover as there was.

Feeling lost in the moment I approached her from behind. I glanced from the bottle in my hand to her arrayed ready for the taking before me.

My gaze drifted from her to her forced viewing of the horizon. It clicked in me what she was trying to do.

She wanted to be mine, but fears of the past were what they were and so she didn't want to look at me and the horizon was something both distracting and beautiful to gaze at.

I wanted her, but something about this just seemed like I would be using her. I didn't want that. And yet, maybe this would break the ice and help her adjust to the thought of me as her lover and not as some replacement of a past abuser.

She was trying very hard to please me and swallowing down my objections I decided to accept the gift for what it was. My hands undid my pants.

I pushed them down enough before then kneeling down before the most welcoming sight I'd ever seen.

Her hands were white knuckled with their grip upon the log and feeling some measure of commiseration for the war she was fighting on my behalf I softly prayed for her courage and enjoyment of what was to come. Opening the bottle I poured the oil into my hand and slicked it down my shaft that was raging for the completion it saw stretched out in open welcome before me.

Consolingly I laid one hand on her back and she jumped slightly. Moving slowly I rubbed the leftover oil into the skin of her lower back even as I pressed an oily finger into her vagina from behind.

She ducked her head down and then once more brought it up to stare at the horizon as I eased my oily finger gently in and out of the very snug fit that she was.

She held still for my finger's possession of her and then I added another.

She gripped the log even tighter and began to breathe heavy.

"Easy now! I'm not them. I really care for you." I whispered out commandingly as I rubbed on her back and her tension seemed to back down some.

Then I really felt an urge from within that I needed to capitalize on this moment and so I did.

I eased my now soaked fingers from her tightness and with relish for what was to come I pressed the head of my oiled shaft into her vagina as I used both hands to rub coaxingly up and down her back. She fought to stay still, but I sensed the intense urge to flee from my invasion of her and so I prayed.

I prayed and exercised the most willful restraint of my life by entering her so slowly as to not even be moving. She was so tight though that I truly couldn't have entered much faster than I was doing.

The feeling was intense beyond belief as slowly inch by inch I felt her body force itself to adjust to the girth of my shaft. Gritting my teeth I held back and forced myself to continue feeding her my shaft ever so slowly while whispering endearments to her that I truly meant with all my heart.

My shaft was better than halfway into her glorious tightness when she turned her head away from the horizon to look at me. At first I thought it was all over and the imagined loss of the feel of her about my shaft was almost crushing, but despite the tears on her face I soon saw that she was trying to indicate something much different.

Her attempt at speaking my words failed, but I knew and nodded, even as relief swept through me. She knew it was me now and not somebody from the past.

She glanced forward again and then to my pleasure she began to back up onto my shaft until it was plushly buried to the hilt within her.

She was so tight that I was seeing stars and control now was more difficult than ever.

Her advance upon my shaft stopped and I waited. I waited as the intense urge to move caused sweat to roll down my face in abandon.

Still I waited for her.

Her hands left the log and folding them onto the ground before her she sank her head down and her back arched even deeper for me and I knew I could do everything I wanted to now.

Without hesitation as I gripped a hold of her hips I pulled back only to surge forward into her wet tightness again and again until with a blinding explosion of release I let off everything deep within her as I clutched at her hips trying to force my way in even deeper than I already was.

I was not gentle and yet she pushed back against me with a willing submissiveness to be gored by my shaft that I simply loved her for. Orgasmic surge after surge swept through me as what felt like an eons worth of seed drained from me into her and in complete repletion I slumped over her back to place my hands on the log.

Whispering repeatedly I said, "Thank you, JaLin! Thank you......" All the while she held still accepting all of my deeply pressed shaft into her.

Despite the lethargy of my passions aftermath I pulled at her hair and she lifted her head and turned it to the side and our eyes met. She smiled and in that moment I knew we were going to be all right.

Softly, I praised God for the moment. This was without a doubt the best day of my life and now it would only get better because now I knew I was free to sink my desire into this beautiful girl now my wife again and again whenever I wished to.

What had been a bad day was now one with a new beginning. Reluctantly, I pulled out of her and not being able to resist myself, I leaned forward and kissed both cheeks of her bottom before I pulled her dress back down.

Pulling my own pants up I then helped her to her feet. She had a bashful and yet slightly playful demeanor about her now that I was instantly attracted to.

She was smiling again and with a gesture to my crotch she then spread her hands apart to symbolize something big. Smiling, I surprised her by picking her up in my arms.

"Yes, honey, I am, and you are the perfect home for it!"

With that said I started walking back towards the house as her arm fell to lay easily along the back of my shoulders.

CHAPTER FIVE

Stretched Full

JaLin

JaLin shook her head back and forth and groaned as her hair cascaded about her shoulders. He was so big!

Bigger than any man who had ever had her and yet she'd come to crave his thickness and depth into her innermost being.

He was different than the others. Oh, so very different!

He didn't use her. He made love to her and he cared about her pleasure more than his own it seemed.

Through the passion of being fully seated upon her husband's shaft, she glanced down and took in the erotic sight of his big fingers playing with her feminine bud of pleasure, even as the thickness of his manhood gored her to the hilt.

She had a good view of all he did to bring her to the point of insanity with his endless caresses and insistence upon her orgasming.

She'd already come twice, but for him that never seemed enough. He spoiled her unselfishly and breathing heavy she convulsed tightly upon his deep-seated shaft buried in her, as his finger rubbed repetitively over her bud with the slickness of her inner juices that leaked out around his thick shaft with ever abundant supply.

The pleasure he gave her was so intense it felt simply too much and again she tried to rise up off him, but he made it hard to do.

For one with her thighs split apart over his as he sat on the kitchen chair it didn't leave her the ability to get more than her tip toes to reach the floor to gain any leverage.

The chief limiting factor however was the muscle corded arm of masculine strength that was wrapped around her waist just below her breasts that kept her firmly anchored back against his chest and impaled upon his shaft.

She tossed her head in frustration and inwardly shook with delight as he chuckled deeply into her hair near her ear.

His masculinity overwhelmed her and she just couldn't help her reactions to him as she came again as in her halfhearted struggle to be free, his thick shaft moved about in her, causing a multitude of reactions that shook through her as pleasure and lots of it. Screaming, she begged for him to both make a stop of her torment and for him to never stop what he was doing.

The corded musculature of his large thighs that she sat upon flexed and he stood up carrying her along with him. Easily, he manipulated her with his hands until she found herself hanging face down over the back of his shoulder as he began to walk to the bedroom.

Anticipation for what was to come coursed through her viscerally as she knew he was about to take her hard. She wanted him to!

In truth, she ached for him too. It had been like this for three days now, ever since she had forced herself to accept his shaft while gazing at the horizon.

Ever since then instead of her actions being of self-sacrifice in order to assuage his desire for her the opposite had been true. He had literally showered her with loving attention and pleasure the likes of which she had never known.

Clutching her nails into the muscles of his back, she smiled and feeling completely uninhibited she bit him. Not hard, but enough to notice.

His big hand rubbed over her bottom in a way that was more caress than any retaliation for her actions. He was always giving.

She let go and kissed the spot she had bit even more passionately than she had bitten it. Her lips were pulled away then from his flesh as he unslung her from his shoulder and flipped her forward onto the edge of the bed gracefully.

It was no mistake that she found herself situated on her knees facing away from him. He loved to take her in this way more than any other and she didn't mind at all.

Shuddering, she lost her breath at the sensation of him sliding down to kneel on the floor just past the edge of the bed directly behind her. Her torment wasn't over.

Gripping tight handholds of the coverlet she moaned as his big fingers pulled the tight lips of her womanhood apart for him to slide his tongue up and down her entire slit. The noisiness of his tasting of her was its own erotic thrill and aching for his touch, she pushed against his mouth and the pressure of his licking tongue as he drank her juices.

She felt like her eyes were crossed from the pleasure he forced upon her with his warm tongue and full lips, but more than anything she ached for his shaft to plunge deeply. He had gone from her estimation of being too big to fit to now wanting him as deep as he could put it into her.

His mouth pulled back from her wetness and with a thrill she felt his heavy breath upon her exposed flesh. Then his head moved and he bit one of the cheeks of her bottom.

JaLin shuddered and came again in a small climax that seemed to be jerked from her by the domineering possession of this man's control over her to do whatever he absolutely wanted to. He let go and licked the spot that he had bitten, only to then drag his tongue across and bite her other cheek.

He loved her bottom that she knew and it really wasn't a big surprise to her when his teeth left her other cheek only to then feel his face pressed between both of them and feel his warm wet lips kiss her bottom entrance. The feel of his lips upon her most private entrance sent a sharp tingle down her spine that resulted in a deeply released groan of pleasure.

Knowing that she couldn't take back the admission that he had just pleased her, she knew that inadvertently she had just given him all the permission he needed to go further and it wasn't within her to tell this man no. He was her husband and she was his.

Holding still for her lover's exploration of her bottom she opened her eyes with surprise as the wetness of his tongue came out to touch her tightly crinkled bottom entrance. She'd never had a man touch her here and without a doubt she accepted the fact that one day this man would place his shaft to the hilt in her bottom.

Such a reality was scary and yet his tongue brought unexpected pleasure after pleasure. It was different and yet it felt good and with openness she held her bottom against his face as he stimulated it in a way she'd never of thought possible as to be pleasurable.

His tongue was in her and rubbing her face on the bed, she moaned at the exotic feel of it and then she came as his big fingers came up from beneath to rub upon her clitoris again. Screaming into the coverlet she felt him rise up behind her and in the midst of her outpouring passion she idly wondered into which opening his shaft would plunge.

It plunged into her vagina and with a gasp of both joy and discomfort at the raging size of him she held onto the coverlet beneath her. He held still deep within her and that was when she felt one of his big fingers slick with her juices begin to press into the tightness of her bottom.

Gasping helplessly she felt his finger gain entrance into her bottom almost easily as he had soaked her entrance with his saliva quite thoroughly. Picking her head up off the bed as every muscle within her body seemed to flex she exclaimed, "Ohhhhh!!!" As the most intense feeling of pleasure and of being dominated by her lover swept through her as his muscled finger went all the way in past the tight bands of constricting muscles in a clear testament to the fact that this man, her husband, intended to possess all of her whether she liked it or not, only she did.

She proved it to herself then as she held steady as with one hand splayed over her hip he began to surge his manhood back and forth into her deeply even as one finger on his other hand remained buried deeply between the cheeks of her bottom. The orgasm that had begun at his fingers entrance never stopped.

She gave out breathy exclamation with each surge forward of his thickness within her that was now only intensified all the more by the presence of his finger in her rear. She bit the coverlet then in her impotency to stop the passion rocketing through her only to experience the sensation of his finger starting to move in tune with his shaft and then there was the invading presence into her tight rear of having not just one but two fingers pressing deeply into virgin territory.

The pressure was just too intense and she couldn't take anymore!

Neither could he and together they both crashed over the edge into orgasm. His spewing shaft pressed deep as did his fingers and JaLin felt herself lose all touch with reality as passion swept her into a dreamless realm of sheer joy at having been filled to the full by this man, who cared for her unlike any man ever had before.

CHAPTER SIX

Dessert First

Two Months Later

I hurried the last bit of the way to the house's yard gate. Nothing stirred, but then Robbie barked and came lumbering from the house and I relaxed.

I eased inside the gate and let myself pet Robbie affectionately for a long moment before turning to look back over the way I had just come. Things were getting bad in town.

Bad wasn't really the word for it actually. The situation was unsustainable.

The increasingly odd proclivities of the town's populace had taken a turn for the worse. Several children had gone missing and they'd been missing for a while.

Not orphanage children, but outside townsfolk children.

I'd noticed right away several days ago that there weren't as many children around, but not a soul had made mention of the fact of there being an absence of any note worthiness.

In fact, everyone had seemed almost sedated as if enjoying something of hidden significance.

The notion of what could've happened made my stomach churn. Pastor had met my knock at the door today with my loaned gun tucked behind his back.

He knew as little as I did about the missing children and yet I could tell that he was refusing the inevitable conclusion that one must surely come to and yet he knew something was very wrong just the same.

The fact of the matter was that the inhabitants of the town just weren't themselves anymore. I blamed the government food primarily, but there were many factors to consider, but chiefly it all boiled down to one thing.

The children needed to get out of town!

Pastor had agreed wholeheartedly to that and to that end he was readying them even now to slip out of town tonight. It was a full moon and so there would be plenty of light to see by.

It would be a harrowing march all the same for the kids, which is why I was going back. I'd had to leave for appearance's sake, but also because it was needful in order to once more don the trappings of a past that I'd wanted nothing else but to leave behind for forever.

It was time to be a warrior again.

Going to the house I stepped inside to see JaLin bringing something out of the oven. Her face was beaming as she viewed the contents of the dish before her.

I smiled wryly at the look of pleasure on her face. I'd never seen a woman make do with so little to go on in terms of food to cook.

Nevertheless, she somehow derived pleasure from just the simplest recombination of the bland vegetables I was able to get to grow.

She glanced up and her smile for me was truly heartwarming, but then it faded as her eyes studied me more closely. She set the hot dish down and coming to me she queried softly to me in her language.

Though I didn't understand her words I still got the question of them. I gestured with a thumb over my shoulder towards the town and said, "It's bad. Kids are missing and it's not good. The kids from the orphanage need to come here." I said, pointing to the floor and she nodded emphatically.

Being in agreement was good. Very good and I relaxed a little, but not much as the prospect of tonight and the days afterward were wearing on me heavily.

JaLin came to me and her face wore a look of commiseration that soothed my worries enough for me to confess, "I've got a bad feeling. It might be over for us soon. I just don't know what will happen. Sometimes I think it's just the memory of former years that's all that keeps the people in town together. Right now, though they frankly scare me. I'm not ashamed to admit it either! I've been in war and I've seen something like this before. It's not good and I don't like where I think it's going to end. I'm only one man and there's a whole town full......."

Her hands stilled my lips from speaking further. She shook her head negatively and pressed against my heart with one hand before jumbling out, "You able to fight good."

Despite the situation, I smiled and said, "I understood that!"

She smiled, but her seriousness came back and taking her hand, she smashed her fist into the palm of the other one in a surprisingly violent action and then pointing to me she surprised me further by saying with heavy inflection, "Warrior!"

A warm glow suffused throughout my entire being as her words coursed through me like a wave of warmth. She believed in me and I loved her all the more for it.

She came close and rising up on tiptoe, she kissed me. I kissed her back as I slid my hands around her tiny waist to hug her to me.

My kiss upon her upturned lips was hungry, but I pulled back with surprise as I felt her hands undo my pants only to then wrap around my thick shaft possessively. I glanced down to see for myself only to witness her glide down to her knees before me until her face was directly poised in front of my cock.

This was something new for her. I wasn't really expecting it, but at the same time I was silently begging for it to go further and then it did.

Her pretty lips kissed the head of my shaft that her hands held and then they separated apart to envelop over the head of my cock as she encased the tip of my cock in the honey warmth interior of her wet mouth.

This was a new progressive step for her forward and silently I basked in the moment. I closed my eyes and gripped my hand over the back of a nearby chair as her lips glided back and forth upon me.

I'd wanted this from her, but I hadn't wanted to ask and now it was all the more special because she was giving it of her own free will. I slid my eyes open only to behold her almond shaped gaze fixed upon me as she played with my cock in her mouth.

"I really like what you're doing, JaLin. Thank you!" I said meaningfully.

Somehow I felt her smile as much as I saw it as her mouth closed over even more of my shaft than it had before. One of her hands came up to massage and lightly squeeze upon my balls and I moaned and swelled even thicker into her mouth.

Silently, I stood there as if rooted to the spot as her mouth moved pleasurably upon me until there was no holding back and I spewed my seed into her mouth. Opening my eyes, I took in the sight of her looking up at me with a gleam of satisfaction within her enigmatic gaze.

Feeling lightheaded I idly watched as she pulled her mouth free of me only to then lick along my shaft to clean up what she'd missed in terms of my spewed forth essence. I so didn't deserve this woman!

Her task done, she made to stand up and I helped her. She fastened my pants back together and still a bit dreamy I let her direct me to sit down in a chair at the kitchen table.

Food was served and as was customary I prayed a blessing over it, only I added an extra note of thanksgiving this time.

She gave a giggle and looking up from the prayed words I'd just said we both smiled at each other and then together took a bite of the food.

The food was awful!

Struggling to not let on, I forced myself to chew it anyway.

Risking a glance her way I saw her gazing at the food on her plate in disgust. She caught my gaze and making a quite bold gesture she pointed to my crotch and then to the food in a way as to say that I tasted better than what she had to eat before her.

I half choked on the food in my mouth before gratefully spitting it out. She rose up quickly and took my bowl away.

Coming back to the table for her bowl I snared her and brought her to me as I remained seated. Glancing up into her frustrated gaze I said, "You know, I bet you'll taste even better still."

Her face flushed, but she was unresisting as I lifted her up to sit on the table's edge. I pushed on her chest and slowly she lay back upon the table, even as I eased her skirt upward.

Stroking my hands along her bare legs I admired the visual treat that she was. She was mine and possessively I lowered my mouth to taste of her feminine beauty.

She shivered in my grasp of her legs as my lips made contact with her. I smiled as I ruminated on the fact that sometimes one got to have dessert before dinner.

Now was such a time and I relished both the taste of her and the sounds of her impassioned moans of pleasure more so than the finest of foods.

I spelled, "*I love you.*" upon her pleasure bud just forward of her sheath with my tongue and then I spelled it all over again and at long last she came.

Her orgasm brought even more increased wetness, but I contented myself with spelling her name in the same fashion as I had just written out my love for her.

She responded violently and chuckling I pressed on with my lovingly done torment of her. My utter intent was to spoil this woman with pleasure.

How could I not when just the sight of her breathed meaning into my life.

Going to the wall of the shed I took off the sledgehammer that hung there. The sun had begun to sink low on the horizon and that meant it was time to leave.

Purposefully, I walked towards my oldest and longest producing raised planting bed. JaLin followed along quite curious.

Staring introspectively at the dirt and its growing produce I made the finality of rediscovering the past by swinging the sledgehammer. The heavy metal head of the hammer splintered apart the wooden boards of the corner of the raised bed and without ceremony, I proceeded to the other three corners and did the same.

Dirt collapsed off to the sides in a cascade leaving in its wake the rise of a perturbed mound in the center of the old planting bed. Stepping through the dirt I began to sweep the dirt off the long crate until I had mostly unearthed it.

Grabbing a handle I pulled hard and drug the crate free of the loose dirt and out to the dry dirt of the plain. Flipping the latches up I opened the lid and exposed to the light what I had buried over six years before.

At that time this planting bed had been for flowers, but now the time for flowers and vegetables was over even as war was likely to begin soon.

JaLin came close and peered in with curiosity to see what was in the crate. I watched as her eyes scanned over the weaponry, medals, uniforms, and general accoutrements of a soldier.

I waited patiently until her eyes rose to mine and I asked, "Still like me?"

Her brow wrinkled and pressing a hand to my heart, she made it clear that she did. I let out a breath and turned back to the crate and said, "That's good. Because if you only knew how many of your religious sect I've put an end to things might be different."

She said nothing, and yet somehow I doubted she'd missed the meaning of what I'd said. She stayed and even helped me put on the gear of a former life as if my past didn't bother her at all. A past that was bathed in bloodshed.

There had been no respectable place for a killer in the society of past years, but now things were different. Now it seemed like I was the last truly free person left alive that I knew of.

Carefully inspecting over the Lapua 50 caliber sniper rifle that I had carried for years and made most of my kills with I discovered that it was in fine working order just as I had left it. The bolt moved easily with no sign of rust or hesitation. It was ready to kill again and sadly so was I.

I slid the rifle over my shoulder along with my other lighter assault rifle before turning my gaze to JaLin. Tears were streaming down her face and not knowing how to make it any easier on her I stepped forward and kissed her passionately before quickly moving away at a jog for the gate and the town beyond.

I glanced back once only to see the JaLin had fallen to her knees in the dirt of the torn apart planting bed.

"Please keep her safe, God!" I whispered even as I moved on. In just a short time I'd found the love of my life and the thought of never seeing her again hurt in a way that threatened me as if it was an armed foe bent upon my complete destruction.

CHAPTER SEVEN

Soulless

I moved stealthily closer and closer to the town ever being acutely aware that if what I thought was really happening to the townspeople was in fact a reality than they may very well be out hunting in an effort to feed their new feralness of nature.

That I had not come across any sign of Pastor and the children was also of great concern to me as I had expected them to be gone from the town already.

I smelled smoke!

Forgoing caution I moved forward at a run up the last rise that lay between me and the town and there I stopped in horror as I took in the sight of the church wreathed in flames.

What was even worse was the imagery of the townsfolk parading about the church in a circling shuffle as if in replication of some bygone pagan ritual of child sacrifice from the ages of antiquities dark past.

Screams rang out through the air from the children inside the burning church and yet the shifting mob outside only shuffled about faster as they threw their hands up into the air as if in worship of something unseen.

Not a child at all now remained among the ranks of the townspeople that had gone mad. Overcome by both the loss of the townspeople's human identity and the searing wrath at such an action of burning children alive I unslung my sniper rifle along with the less bulky assault rifle that I carried as a companion weapon.

I snapped down the tripod legs of the 50cal. and unslung the bandolier studded with its oversized ammo from off my shoulder.

Crouching down I laid out flat and slipped off the caps of the night vision scope mounted to the rifle.

The scene came instantly alive to me through the reticle of the scope. The back door of the church opened and smoke billowed out through it. Pastor stumbled out, followed along by the children.

Through the scope I saw that he had my gun in hand, but their appearance was what the others had been waiting for. The circling shuffle abruptly stopped and in mass the townspeople held up bloody knives and axes and screamed in glee.

Pastor started shooting those closest to him, but it did nothing to deter the demented newly formed cannibals of their own kind from wishing to taste human flesh once more.

I breathed out and squeezed the trigger.

The rifle bucked against my shoulder like an old friend's handshake. The bullet tore off with enough mass and velocity to rip through an armored vehicle or penetrate the concrete wall of a house.

It savagely compacted with flesh once human, but now forsaken of by its soul and tore through it to pierce through the bodies of four others as blood sprayed about everywhere, only to be followed by eruptions of flesh and blood to the right and left as I continued squeezing the trigger on newly stacked up lines of opponents.

The demented charge upon the coughing children faltered as the need for survival dimly registered within the animal like morass of their minds as more and more of them went down both singularly and in groups of screaming agony.

I loaded a new mag and I continued to pull the trigger without compunction or remorse of any kind and I wrecked a heavy toll within seconds upon a town gone mad with the desire for the flesh of innocent children.

Every last one of these self-created monsters could go to hell!

The 50cal. once more empty I picked up my lighter rifle and open sighted I sent round after round into the scattering flock of hopeless cowards. My shots scored heavily and the ground around the church became bathed with blood and the bodies of those who had forsaken their faith.

The children were past the gore and moving in on my position. The older ones were carrying the smaller ones and Pastor had his arms wrapped around two as he headed the group up in making for my position as fast as they could all go without leaving any behind.

Silently, I prayed that the older man didn't have a heart attack. My gun clicked empty and I rolled to my side to access another 30 round mag for it.

An arrow shaft slammed into the ground where I had just been even as wild yells erupted from behind me. I kept rolling and in an adrenalized motion I surged up to my feet as the new mag snapped home within the rifle.

I let the crossbow archer readying another arrow have it several times over, but then the others were on me and I had no more time to shoot.

Holding my rifle up I deflected the down stroking blade of an axe.

I kicked the screeching assailant in the belly and sent him flying backwards, even as I shoved the butt of the rifle with brutal force trauma several inches into the face of a machete wielding psycho off to my right.

Dodging away from the dying man's machete strike I kept moving fast and slipped away from the stabbing touch of a woman's outthrust butcher knife at me.

Smoothly I leaned forward and whipped up the strap of my rifle and it looped over the woman's head and as it fell about her neck I twisted the rifle, bringing the strap tight then as she tried to stab at me again, I kept the momentum going and abruptly tugged on my rifle in a twisting motion that took the woman off her feet and snapped her neck.

She fell down dead and I unloosed my strap from off her neck.

Stepping backward I pulled the trigger and let the recovering axe man that I now recognized as the former postmaster have it several times.

He collapsed and his out flung axe fell so close it nearly landed on my foot.

Two more of the pack remained and like the undecided rats of nature that they had become they waffled about whether to attack or run. I took care of the decision for them and as they fell bleeding to the ground I spun back to see what had become of the children.

They came huffing into view and with relief I saw that no one from the town had dared to pursue. Swinging back to cover my back, I scanned the area, but nothing moved in the dark.

Sounding completely overcome Pastor stumbled to his knees nearby and let go of the two kids he had carried free of the town. I swung my rifle over my shoulder, but thought better of it as I saw a boy of about twelve reach down to pick up a fallen machete and then with it gripped tensely turn to stare back at the town now brightly illuminated in the night by the church engulfed in flames.

"Here put that thing down." I said, approaching the boy and extending him my rifle.

He took it from me with shock and I said, "Just pull the trigger and it will go boom. You take up the rear and you shoot anything that moves you hear me?"

The boy nodded white faced and quickly moved back to the rear of the group. He had the fine makings of a soldier or at the very least a survivor.

I slung my 50cal. up off the ground and reloaded it. Holding it level at my waist with one hand, I extended the other down to the still out of breath man who had fought so hard to give these kids a chance.

Wearily, Pastor took my hand and I pulled him up to his feet. Our eyes met and dimly we nodded at each other as if in confirmation of the common knowledge of the war we were in for from this moment onward.

"Alright everyone, this way." I said, as I began to lead the group off through the moonlit darkness for home even as the last vestige of civilized order burnt to the ground in the town behind us.

They would be after us soon enough. While they had plenty to eat for the moment the evil nature that they had given place to wouldn't be satisfied for any longer than a few passing moments.

The farm was not safe, indeed nowhere would be safe for us, but at least if we were on the move, then there was at least something better in terms of a chance happening to benefit us in terms of going in our favor.

I'd let the kids sleep for a few hours once we reached the homestead, but before the sun was up we would be moving on.

It was too cold towards the North, nothing to the South appealed to me and from eyewitness accounts the West was even worse than the town that lay behind me. That left the East.

It was all that was left in terms of an option and dying of cancer right now didn't seem like such a compromise as opposed to being chewed upon by my own kind.

~~~~~~~~~

The night wore on and it took longer than I had thought it would to reach the house and when we did no light greeted us.

I held the group up and listened, but I heard nothing.

Fear began to eat away at my insides as if it was an animal bent on destroying me.

"Stay here!" I ordered gruffly, as I made my way forward through the gloom of late night.

At any moment I expected to be pierced through by a scalp hunter's arrow, but the night remained eerily silent.
~~~~~~~~~

I made my way through the gate that hung open into the yard surrounding the house.

A breeze drifted across the yard and with it a telltale tuft of white hair. I stopped and let my gaze follow along to where I made out the bloody and mostly picked clean carcass of what had once been Robbie.

Most of him was gone and all that remained was hair and bones. Cold sweat squeezed from my pores and with dread I stepped out toward the darkened house that bore the evidence of smashed windows and a general air of disruption of what had once been good.

Stepping inside with my finger on the trigger I stepped over upturned chairs and debris laying all about upon the floor. The room had been torn apart and from my view all vestige of food in the kitchen was gone.

The floor was littered with broken glass and my boots crunched through it as I made my way through it and stepped into the bedroom. The room was dark, but my eyes saw no sign of the remains of a body.

Relief was far from me though. Where was JaLin?

I left the bedroom and made my way upstairs only to find more destruction, but the absence of JaLin or any sign of her. Going back downstairs, I reentered the bedroom.

Going to the bed I let my rifle fall onto it. I lost it then and crashing down onto my knees beside the bed I felt the intense pain of a loss too great as to ever be put into words as my body was wracked by deep sob after sob.

Reaching out I grabbed her pillow up and burying my face in it, I breathed in the smell of her and I cried all the harder.

"Oh God kill me now! I...... it would be a mercy!" I begged through my tears.

The floor squeaked behind me and the routine of training took over and one-handed I swung the rifle up as I spun around prepared to fill whatever it was with bullets, but there was nothing.

The floor squeaked again and blinking I swung the barrel of the rifle to a spot where the floor was moving!

It was my ammo cache spot!

Crawling across the floor I ripped away the snug fitting boards of the cache location to take in the sight of JaLin completely folded over on herself in an impossibly tiny space.

"Oh God!" I exclaimed, as I pulled her out of the hole that I wouldn't have thought large enough for even a small child to fit into let alone a woman of her size. Not only that, but she'd been like this for hours!

Coming unfolded in my arms, she breathed in deeply with a gasp and stretched out as much as she could, all the while trembling with what I recognized as pain.

I could only imagine how she felt. Glancing at the tiny hole I puzzled on the fact of how she'd even closed the floor boards back over top of herself.

I rubbed at her back and legs as she sat on the floor beside me and all the while I thanked God over and over again that she was alive. Having recovered her breath and some degree of mobility she turned her head to me and with tears falling she whispered, "Robbie."

Nodding my head, I pulled her to me as my own tears fell.

"He fight hard." She said brokenly before adding, "Gave me time."

I nodded and kissed the top of her head. Gathering her to me I got up.

With her face buried against my neck I made it to the bed and awkwardly picked up my rifle. Managing it and her I headed for the door.

Along the way out of the house I said, "What do you think about us naming our first boy Robbie?"

She breathed out the word for '*yes*' in her language against my neck even as she kept her eyes averted from anything she might see in the yard. I made it to Pastor and the children and Pastor shouldered the big 50cal. for me.

Without a word said I led the way off towards the East all the while gaining strength from each breath of having the sensation of my woman alive and well in my arms. Hours went by and now she walked by my side, but still we traveled on as the sun rose in the sky.

We walked due East through the abandoned countryside seeing no one and that was good, because my tendency of the moment right now was to shoot first and ask questions later.

That was one of the problems with the war to survive. It had a tendency to make monsters of us all.

CHAPTER EIGHT

"Say it!"

Cradling the heavy 50cal. in my arms I scouted ahead as the group of children rested back behind me. Our needs were simple.

We needed water and secondarily food as the vandals had left nothing alive in my raised planting beds. Typical of humanity gone over the edge to destroy the very plants that could have born them even more food if left alive.

Although our needs were simple they were becoming increasingly dire by the moment. Thankfully though I had an outlet to express my needs.

"God, Your Word says you know what our needs are before we do so…. well…. help please."

I crested over the top of a ridge and glanced down with surprise at what lay below me. I stood still and watched long and thoughtfully upon the abandoned looking homestead located below.

A pond of water stood off to the one side of the house and offered the promise of fulfillment for the raging thirst I had acquired. I stayed where I was though in indecision.

The place looked long abandoned.

Finally, I expressed my fears to my Creator, "Is it safe?"

"Yes, son." Came an affirming response from within my soul, but not willing to be tricked at this stage of the game I tested the voice by Scripture to ascertain that I wasn't being tricked because to me there seemed to be a demonic theme to the personification of darkness that I beheld in almost everything these days.

My doubts, however were cast aside though as I received confirmation that I was indeed speaking to a representative of the Spirit of God and I headed back for the others, even as a warmth from within spilled throughout me and said, **"Well done, son."**

~~~~~~~

JaLin's mouth was dry, but looking over at Pastor she wouldn't be denied from speaking any longer as to what she knew had occurred. She wanted to make sure.

Reaching over she shook his shoulders slightly and tiredly, his eyes opened with alarm.

"No, no, nothing to fear. I…. I want to talk. May I?" JaLin asked respectfully.

Pastor Joseph straightened up from leaning back against a rock and said fluently within her own language, "Of course you can."

She looked away, but then back to him as a bubble of joy lit her up from within, "Last night I prayed to your God. I know He is God. I know this. I didn't know though if He wanted me. I thought maybe He would as why would He give me to such a good man like Adam and…… but anyway…." JaLin paused as remembered angst came back to her in full force.

Pastor Joseph put a consoling hand over top of hers and squeezed and suddenly very emotional JaLin met his kind gaze and said, "I thought I would die! I had to hide and the only place they not look would be in the floor and so I tried to fit into the space, but I couldn't! I couldn't!!!" She pressed heavily in exclamation and Pastor nodded knowingly.

"I prayed. Not to my people's false god, but to Adam's God and God's Son, Jesus. I……" JaLin's voice trailed off and Pastor pressed, "What happened next, JaLin?"

Wiping at her eyes that felt like they should be crying, but lacked the moisture to do so she said, "The wood moved. It moved and I fell
~~~~~~~

into the spot like I was made smaller and yet I'm still my size. I'm too big to have fit into the floor!"

Pastor nodded, smiling and asked, "Is that all?"

"No, the floor pieces slid over top of me and clicked down into place. I never touched them. It was so tight in the hole. I couldn't breathe and then the Man, Jesus, He came to me somehow and He said, *"I'll breathe for you, JaLin. Tomorrow I want you to complete your journey, but for now I'm here and I love you and you're going to be all right."* I felt such peace at His saying of that and truly I don't remember anything else until I heard Adam's voice in the bedroom."

Then moving onto her knees before Pastor she asked, "What is it I should do now? I know your God is real. I want to serve Him like you and Adam do. I want His Spirit in me like Adam has and like I see in your eyes. What do I do?"

Pastor took her hands in his and said, "Well JaLin it's actually very simple. You believe in Jesus, that He is God's only begotten Son?"

"I do."

"Do you know that when Jesus died for you on a cross a long time ago that when He did so He took your sins and everyone else's to the grave, but that after three days' time He rose from the grave because death couldn't conquer Him?"

"I believe you. I've seen Him. He could do anything!" JaLin said earnestly.

"Well then, even as Jesus died for your sins, will you confess yourself as a sinner and ask Him to forgive you and ask for His Father's Holy Spirit to come into you and make you forever from now on a child of God and an heir to spending all of eternity in His Father's presence forever more with Him?"

"I do!" JaLin said emotionally.

"Say it." Pastor encouraged.

"I want you in my life, Jesus! Please forgive me for everything I've done wrong. I want you! I need Your Father's Spirit like I see it in Adam! Please save me, teach me, and make me Yours for forever!"

Pastor was smiling and squeezing her hands as she dissolved into tears of joy he said, "Your His now JaLin! Nothing can ever separate you from His love for you! Not death, no, not anything! Your story no longer ends at the grave. You're free JaLin. Free!"

Crying as the full knowledge of that swept through her JaLin pressed her hands to her face and cried joyfully as the children looked on with teary-eyed faces that bespoke of the joy that they shared with JaLin, because of the Pastor's example to them which had fostered the same spiritual maturation in them that she now had with God.

Even though the conversation had taken place in a language different from their own they full well comprehended what had just occurred and despite their tiredness they pressed close and hugged their arms about JaLin and Pastor.

Pastor Joseph looked upwards to the bright sky overhead and in English said, "It's going to be a great day! Wouldn't you agree, Adam?" He said at the last, glancing over at me to where I stood as a silent witness to the exchange that had occurred between him and JaLin and I nodded my head as tears of my own streaked down my face.

"Yes, Sir! It certainly is!" I affirmed.

JaLin's head picked up at the sound of my voice and rising up, she waded through the children until she got to me. Her arms swept around me and I hugged her to me fiercely.

We stood that way for a long moment as more joy than I had known in a long time seemed to inflect the day with its cheer as it washed away all the horrors of the night and the days of our time.

Tipping her head back, she gazed up at me out of those beautiful almond shaped eyes of hers and haltingly said in English, "I love you, Adam."

I'd heard her say, '*I love you*', in her language to me many times as I had lain partially asleep at night and doing my very best to replicate the sounds of her oft repeated phrase at night, when she thought I was asleep, I said, "*I love you.*"

To my own ears, I'd totally botched the tonal frequencies of her language, but she knew and with a desperate cry, she pulled on my shoulders and I lifted her so that we could kiss and for a moment her love for me totally dominated the kiss, until I showed her with equal desire that I felt just the same about her.

If the children hadn't been present we would've celebrated love and new spiritual life in an entirely different fashion, but as it was we contented ourselves with the knowledge of the life that we would spend with each other from this day forward.

Knowing now best of all that death no longer held any sway over our futures and so if we had a week, an hour, or a hundred years it didn't matter. We had right now and thanks to Jesus we didn't have to fear the eternity to follow.

Life had never been fuller or sweeter than it was in this moment and I thanked God intensely for it over and over in my spirit as I continued to hold onto the priceless gift from a Father who knew what I needed most of all. Even in the midst of the hell of our circumstances His eternal will reigned supreme and in no way had it been overcome.

CHAPTER NINE

Reality Check

I felt along the wire as I traced it to its source within the engine compartment. Thankfully, my fingers encountered nothing but cobwebs and old grease.

The wire was intact. That at least made one for once.

I pulled my arm out of the engine compartment. Picking up a rag I stepped back from the Mustang and surveyed my handiwork.

I'd had to replace most of the wiring as mice had made piecemeal of things underneath the hood, but theoretically things should work now. I'd changed the oil yesterday, along with the gas.

The oil really hadn't needed to be changed, but the supplies were available and so why not. Indeed, it had been nice to do something of such a former pastime as working on a car again with the pursuit to drive it.

It wasn't the only thing I wanted to drive though. Reaching forward I took the hood extension rod down and snapped it flat into place and then I let the hood slam down.

With the hood closed I turned my back to the car and faced my silent admirer, who had perched herself on top of a barrel nearby. She smiled and eyed me over speculatively as I continued to wipe my hands off on the rag.

I had never known or even heard of the existence of this place that lay within a two-day walk of my own place and yet there was good reason for it. It was a bug out homestead.

There wasn't even a noticeable road other than a leveled off dirt path leading away from this place. The house and the shed were fully stocked with all the food and necessities needed to make it in a grid down situation and to some degree quite luxuriously.

Whoever had set this place up hadn't made it though and for the past two years or so it had sat here waiting. Waiting to fulfill a desperate need in a feat of God appointed timing that was undeniable.

I had not ceased to praise God for the provision of this place and truly a stockpile of food capable of lasting years, if managed correctly. It was exactly what Pastor and the kids needed.

In short, this place bought us some time, but I wasn't satisfied with that alone. I needed to know if things further out were as bad as I had been told that they were.

To that end, I intended to explore and test the waters so to speak. I wanted to do it alone, but JaLin wouldn't have it.

She'd broken through my hard reserve to her coming along yesterday by stating in English, "You live, I live. You suffer, I suffer. You die, I die. You go, I go!"

I'd given it up then. There was simply no denying a plea played on the heartstrings such as that.

Speaking of hearts - I idly took in the way her nipples were peaked hard against the t-shirt she wore. Her breasts were small, but I didn't care. They were still quite fun to play with and highly responsive.

I reached out an oil stained hand and rubbed it over one of them possessively and had the satisfaction of watching her eyes blink closed for a moment. They opened again with a ready fire within them to experience more and I was helpless to fight against the urge to make her passions come true.

I glanced toward the shed's access door only to have my eyes drawn back to JaLin as she held up a key in the air. I smiled wolfishly and stepping close I bent my head to hers and whispered, "You little vixen you! You want me that bad do you?"

She nodded her head emphatically before then kissing me. I kissed her back even as I let my hands slide down her back to squeeze over her rounded little bottom.

I picked her up and her arms and legs closed around me. I then carried her through the garage a short distance never breaking the kiss with her and then I laid her down.

Her eyes opened as our lips parted and with a bit of a smirk she took in the fact that I had just laid her down on the hood of the Mustang. I grinned right back at her as I pulled her shoes off and then her tight jeans along with her T-shirt.

I'd always wanted to do this with a girl and now I got to do it with my girl. She wore a dazed expression of wanton desire as I pressed her legs up and apart even as I kneeled down onto the concrete floor.

The floor was hard, but I didn't care. The experience of doing this was worth it.

My mouth descended upon the slick wetness that her womanhood already was and I took my fill of her as I sought to drive her to a fever pitch of wanton need. Moaning and twisting about upon the hood, she accepted the strokes of my tongue upon her and when she was breathing heavy and almost over the edge I stopped.

She moaned in anguish and chuckling I got up and undid my pants. Her passioned eyes took in the desire for her that I always had before they rose to my eyes with open want for all I had to offer.

I grasped her ankles and slid her lower down on the hood until her bottom was poised slightly over the edge. I split her legs apart and rested them against my shoulders as I bent down over her and placed my oily hands to either side of her on the car hood.

Her feet caressed my neck and ears as I familiarly nuzzled my shaft into her tight folds. Holding her gaze, I pushed forward into drive and watched to see how she would respond.

Her nails bit into my sides and her groan was answer enough to testify that she was ready to ride and so I did. She was fast and came hard and moments later I joined her and she fell over the edge with me for a second time.

Breathing heavily from the exertion of past moments I held my weight up off of her. That said, I still stayed fully connected with her, as it simply felt good just to be in her.

Glancing about introspectively I came to the conclusion that I had dented the hood. Oh well.

My eyes met hers and she knowingly squeezed down on my shaft with her strong inner core muscles.

Groaning, I shook my head. She was amazing and I told her so on the spot.

Her hand came up to caress my cheek, "You too." She said.

I let her feet slide off my shoulders and letting down onto my elbows I kissed her. I loved this woman so much!

We stayed that way kissing for a while and then she curled her legs up around me and ground herself against me. Unbelievably, I felt myself stiffen to full hardness again within her tight sheath and I started to drive her all over again much to her delight.

~~~~~~~~

We'd said our farewells which were hopefully only temporary. Now, however the moment of truth had come.

I turned the key and the engine came alive and purred like a throaty kitten ready to catch a ride on a fast-moving stallion.

I'd started the car earlier, when I'd flushed the old gas out of it, but the sound of power willing to move never got old after being absent from the world of familiar sounds such as it had been for almost three years.

No, this was nice, as were the sunglasses I wore. I glanced to JaLin only to see her likewise enjoying the experience.
~~~~~~~~

Truth to be said I was glad that she was coming along. It was hard to say what fate lay before us, but it was better knowing that we would face it together.

I gave Pastor Joseph and the kids a wave and then I eased the car forward down the dirt level track being mindful of the roughness of the terrain. The dirt only lasted for about a mile and then we were pulling up onto the abandoned tarmac of a paved road unused to the sound of power on four wheels in a while.

Sand had blown across the road here and there along with other debris, but I didn't let it block me from achieving my pursuit and intense need for speed. I looked behind me at the towering rise of stirred up dust. It was a glorious sight.

What we were headed into I didn't know, but the expectation of the unknown threatened to drive me nuts almost as much as the desire occurred to me to pull over and enjoy my wife all over again. She must've read my sideways glance at her because her hand came out across the seats and began to possessively rub over my crotch that immediately bulged into her massaging touch upon it.

She didn't stop and my torment continued. I was on the verge of pulling over when her hand undid my pants.

My shaft busted threw the gap that she had opened. Her hand withdrew from touching me and I had started to look her way when I heard a '*click*'.

My gaze settled on her only to see her seatbelt receding away. She turned in her seat and coming close to me as she knelt in her seat she pressed her lips wetly into my ear.

Pulling back slightly, she took her sunglasses off. Taking one of my hands off the steering wheel she said, "Hold please." And I did just that.

Her head lowered and I groaned before her lips ever touched the head of my cock, only to then experience more pleasure, as she began to suck lightly upon my shaft. No, this day simply couldn't get any better.

I glanced about helplessly as pleasure radiated up-and-down me on multiple levels as she stroked her mouth up and down on the essence of who I was as a male. There were no words to describe this moment, but I did my best to anyway.

"Thank you so much, God!"

Keeping on the road brought a new challenge to me in the face of what was happening, but I did it all the while planning within my mind as to how on earth I could ever return as much significance in pleasure to her as she was giving to me right now. My mind, however, came up with nothing that could equal with what she was doing and at about the same time my body gave up to the inevitable.

Gripping the wheel hard I breathed heavily as she continued to suck on me hotly through the heat of my passion and groaning, I kept us on the road just barely as her mouth worked hungrily upon me. Never would I suggest this for the safety of others, on the road, but we were alone out here and yet I'd do it again even with other cars.

Her head rose up and my eyes took in the arousal to be found in hers and something bade me to speak out and in as authoritative of a voice as I could muster in the moment, I said, "I want you to come right now."

To my surprise, she did.

Her hips jerked and she pressed her face into my neck as she cried out softly as her own passions swelled to a high pitch of accomplished yearning.

After a long moment she pulled away and I held her sunglasses out to her. How I had avoided from crushing them, I did not know, but I was happy that I hadn't.

She put them on and slid back into her seat and redid her seatbelt. The sun had fully risen in the morning sky and the road was open and clear before us.

I settled down to about 80 mph as I enjoyed literally everything going on in the moment, but most of all the sense of loving connection I shared with JaLin that topped all else. Our hands lay clasped together near the gear shifter and they stayed that way as mile after mile of barren landscape fell off behind us.

~~~~~~~

Truly the FEMA people had been right, at least that is how it seemed.

I was driving through yet one more long night and I had already resolved to turn around and head back once the sun began to rise up over the horizon.

I had just enough gas to make it most of the way back.

There was no end seemingly to the desolation of the land and its former occupants and I was tired of discovering more of the same. Suddenly though I noticed something different in the dark of the night off in the distance.

Lights?

Lots of lights!

The moon was bright and I'd been driving without headlights as I didn't want to announce myself too much and now I continued on doing so. Reaching out a hand, I gently shook JaLin awake.

She sat up quickly and stared transfixed at the lights that lay along the horizon even as I found myself doing the same. Why so many lights?

How were so many lights being powered when it came down to that?

I didn't know, but I intended to find out.

Saying a quiet prayer I eased on forward toward the wall of lights on the horizon. The lights soon revealed that indeed there was a wall. A wall of barbed wire.

I let my one hand fall down beside the door to grip hold of my pistol. The road we followed along led up to a brightly illuminated gate that lay situated in the wall of wire.
~~~~~~~

There were actual people standing about too and they weren't wielding butcher knives or clubs. In fact, they all looked as if they'd had a shower today and their uniforms looked as if recently pressed.

What was going on here?

I was motioned to come to a stop and as I did so an officer approached the window. I lowered it while at the same time prepared to lay a hold of my gun and send a shot clear through him and send the car into reverse at a moment's notice if need be.

His words were harsh, "What sector did you two moonlighters slip through? Taking a joy ride out into the Badlands is no joke! It is in no way safe and you're an idiot if you ever do it again, because I for one am sure not going to come out to help you! Now get back into the Goodland and the next time I catch you guys slipping through the border I'll report you!"

I blinked uncertainly, but at the authoritative wave by the officer the gate in the wall of barbed wire opened and I found myself easing the car forward on through it to the other side all the while receiving dirty looks from all the other border guards that stood nearby with automatic rifles in their arms.

Where did all these normal appearing and quite well fed looking people come from all of a sudden?

The East was supposed to be a complete loss, but now in the distance I saw otherwise, as a brightly lit up grid of lights indicated the presence of a city.

JaLin and I looked at each other in consternation. This most definitely had not been what either of us had been told about.

I drove onward with my headlights on.

On my approach to the city I noticed a sudden change in the greenery to either side of us that was so apparent that the human eye could comprehend it even in the darkness of the night. It was surreal to say the least and I found myself wanting to be back out on the barrens as opposed to this unknown plain of existence that we had stumbled into as if waking up from a bad dream.

Trees were passing by quickly and more and more it became apparent to me that there had been no spraying done here. Even more so than that there had been no nuclear fallout as it had been told to us by FEMA.

I'd passed several fans marked FEMA already.

We entered the city and it became abundantly clear that life was going on here as if nothing had ever happened. Socially things appeared even looser than before, but there had been no complete fall of society, as I had witnessed for the past two years to grace any corner of this city of modernity.

It was apparent that food was not limited at all as a million flashing icons for it advertised it almost everywhere one looked. If a wide-ranging natural diet was available why then was FEMA feeding the people of my former area with such stale and likely poisoned food, unless it all was on purpose somehow to drive them nuts in the first place?

What if it were all a big experiment of some kind?

For the past two and a half years I might have been living and striving to survive in some devilish paradigm of a mad scientist's field day of sociological experimentation.

These people that walked to and fro everywhere one looked, even at night in this city, seemed totally impervious to the fact that beyond the wall of wire people were being eaten by each other and that the chief occupation was to hunt down one another in order to scalp off their faces!

Anger seethed hotly through me and as if sensing it JaLin laid a hand on my arm consolingly. I tamped my emotions down or at least I attempted to.

I pulled the car off the main drag and out of traffic and into a hotel parking lot. Because of a wild inspiration I had actually brought along some money that I'd seen in a drawer at the homestead location just on the possible chance of finding something like this.

Getting out of the car I went to JaLin's side and opened her door for her. She got out and together we walked down the pristine sidewalk with lush green grass growing on either side of it.

Everything about this experience felt unreal.

Entering the immaculately kept hotel lobby, I immediately felt dirty only to have the emotion compounded as everyone present looked up to stare at us. I approached the front desk and was dismissively regarded by the cursory up-and-down glance of the attendant standing there.

Speaking up I said, "I'd like a room for the night. Do you have any available?"

"Quite certainly, Sir. Identification number, please."

I stared at the man blankly for a second before asking, "Do you mean a driver's license?"

The desk clerk's face grew into the smirk that he had been fighting to hold back ever since we'd come in here and succinctly he now said, "I knew it! Another hillbilly rebel come back into civilization's redeeming glow. Yes, you need an identification number. Without it, I'm afraid I can't give you a room and nobody else will either. It's the way things are run now. Society no longer runs on money, but all are free to come and go as they please, as long as they are identified by the number and sworn to all that it stands for. Understood?"

Feeling hollow inside I said, "I see." And then without another word spoken I began to back away from the counter.

Abruptly then I turned and headed for the freedom of the outdoors even as the desk clerk called out, "I'm going to have to report this you know! No one is going to give you food or anything without your personal identification number. Come back here! You won't make it! You've already been biologically scanned and you'll be picked up within hours! You fools...... you can get your number it's super easy!"

The sliding doors of the hotel lobby closed behind us and on a half run, we both made it back to the car and without pause we both jumped in.

The car roared to life and I tore free of the parking lot and the mark of the beast system that had been clearly initiated here in this place of lost souls living on a promise that would only deliver them to hell in the long run.

I would never submit to this spiritual tyranny!

I'd rather die or at the very least spend my life fighting to survive, which is exactly what I intended to keep on doing.

Just short of the border I spotted my ticket to freedom. Roaring up alongside of the white FEMA van making its way toward the wall of lit up barbed wire I forced the van over to the shoulder of the road through aggressive driving.

The FEMA van came to a stop grudgingly and I hopped out of the car gun in hand. The driver of the van had hopped out too, and with angry protest exclaimed, "What's up with you mister? I've got more important things to do than play games like this!"

"Yeah, I know, like feeding hallucinogenic and highly toxic food to unsuspecting people, even as you could've had the ability to feed them almost anything one could ask for from a naturally organic source all along!"

The man had started to draw back in shocked surprise from me, but he wasn't quick enough. I grabbed a hold of him and pulling him close I clubbed him over the head with the gun barrel brutally.

I let him fall to the ground and turning back, I was in time to see JaLin climb free of the car with our bag of provisions in tow.

It was clear that she knew what I intended to do, but I felt like I needed to explain anyway. Pointing to the city of controlled lost souls behind us I said, "I will never accept that mark! I would rather die being fed upon by my own kind than willingly hand over my soul to the devil!"

JaLin nodded her head and pointed to her own heart as well. We were in agreement as man and wife.

I nodded with gratitude for her understanding of how I could turn my back on an easy time of it versus the challenge of having to continue to survive in the barrens beyond the wire in a man-made habitat of horrors.

Truly though there was no horror greater than the intentional loss of the human soul and it was this reality of fallen order that I now wished to escape from the most.

Slipping into the driver seat of the white van I eased it forward even as JaLin made herself scarce by ducking into the back of the van. The border was just ahead and when I reached it the gate opened automatically and without even being asked to stop and verify my shipment of poison the border guards waved me on.

I eased on through the gate and back into the familiarness of the past two years of my life that had seemed to stretch on for an eternity. Now, however seeing the barrens was almost more of a feeling of welcome relief than anything negative in comparison to what we were escaping from.

It was better to die in a day and live for forever in God's presence than it was to prolong an earthly existence for a thousand years only to realize that all that time constituted to nothing more than a day in the span of an equally eternal hell.

I taxed the van as hard as it would go as I fled back into the lands of freedom. Somehow we would make it and if not, then we would die trying.

Relief washed through me as I accepted the scope of what life would be like from now on and the feeling only got better as I felt JaLin's hand squeeze down over my shoulder.

Truly, God had given me everything I needed and I would be content to dwell in it.

I closed my hand over JaLin's hand. Within two days or so we would be back at the homestead with Pastor and the kids and life would go on.

I thanked God on the spot for such a positive future, when before I had railed against the idea of being content in such a make do environment, but now my eyes had been opened and I wasn't ever going to second-guess God again.

In short, I was right where I needed to be in life.

THE END

Dear Reader,

I'm not sure this is a story that can be easily enjoyed as the backdrop of it is quite gritty, but such is life at times and unfortunately most likely the future as well. A story like this is meant to make you think. It was originally written in 2016 (Edit: 2022) and wow – the things that can happen in a few years, huh! The next book in the series, The Will to Thrive is not out yet, but I have enclosed an excerpt from another equally gritty book of mine, Broken but Undefeated. Hopefully you can enjoy it, but more importantly I hope you learn something meaningful from it.

Author's Corner

It would seem that the genre of Erotic Christian Fiction, which I have coined in terms of labeling what I have written, appears to be an entirely new avenue within the Fiction market. Many, who call themselves 'Christian' will not understand what I have taken upon myself to do and in general I expect reactions to what I've written to be hostile and that's okay. Why is that okay? The reason it is okay is because it is better to do what God says then stay hidden safely away within the mass of a group and only do what is perceived amongst the group as 'okay'. Truly the path to hell is paved with both the 'doctrines of man' and 'group think'. I write what I do, because I follow the leading of the Holy Spirit of God and nothing else. This avenue of Christian Erotic themed fiction is something He laid upon my heart to do and I chose to obey the calling and go wherever He wanted it to go. It is within my heart to be obedient to God always and to that end I have gone farther than I ever expected to be asked of me by my God in terms of witnessing to a lost and dying world, but even so, His will be done. If you have questions or comments, please feel free to direct them to me at the following email address: I don't always have answers, but I can pray for you and whatever I can't do – God can.

author-aedan-sayla@proton.me

Thanks for reading and please do leave a review!

Broken but Undefeated

Chapter One

My name is Samira, but I tell no one what it is. I am simply known as, 'Girl 41'.

I once had a last name too, but the world as it is now doesn't care about who you were before everything changed so much as what you are worth now. As girls go I'm worth a lot for at least the time being.

My value can change at any moment though. Part of my allure this far into the game has been the enigmatic poise that I have been able to manifest.

The customers find it enchanting and because of this they pay a lot more for the use of me. They all think that they own me, but they don't.

I'll never be owned.

They can call me a slave. Treat me like a slave. Even kill me if they wish, but inside I will forever be free.

Behind the veil of my eyes is where I truly live. Those that move around me and draw air are empty, while I remain full in a way that their spirits have long since forgotten the meaning of.

At night, as I lay broken from whatever they have done to me, I hear that still small voice from within my soul. A voice of calm loving assurance that tells me that I am loved.

That I matter. That I have value beyond the price that men and women give for the use of my body.

That same voice tells me to hold on over and over again.

It tells my mind to stop its endless wish to kill my own body so that my spirit can truly be free of the endless torment that living has become to mean for me.

It was that voice that I heard spoken through the message of a pastor's sermon every weekend, until the day when the order of civilized society was lost and the great modern chaos of mankind began.

The day when stores no longer had food to sell, even as there was no more money to buy what little there might be left. People soon became one of the new currencies, but in some ways I suppose they were exactly that the whole time, it just wasn't so obvious.

Back then there had been so many distractions and material aplenty that the reality of going back in time in order to escape the harsh realities of the present was little more than a fairytale. In these current days of pressed on chaos only the darkness within the hearts of men seemed to reign supreme.

Truly the darkness had been there before the crash of all the world markets and the famines and pestilences that followed, but never had it seemed so upfront and personal to one and all as it was now.

Wars raged across the world in rapid succession one right after the next. Countries fought over resources only to then see those same resources squandered in the altercation meant to seize them.

The world, as it once was, died and in its place arose a new foreboding era of darkness. An era were all innocence had been lost and where the weak were literally fed upon in the wreckage of cities that had once been home to millions but now only held a desperate few.

In many ways I should count myself more fortunate than my immediate family. My father in order to feed himself and my mother had sold me for a month's worth of rations.

One could only imagine what he had resorted to the next month to feed himself after having done what he had to me. I at least was fed regularly and if my parents were still alive I very much doubted that they could say the same.

That fateful and soul shattering parting from my own family had been a year or more ago now. Truly, I lost track of time.

Maybe it had been two years ago now.

The torment of being at the mercy of the continued abuse by others tended to drive out everything else but the will to survive. One either maintained control or went stark raving mad.

There were no girls left in the rotation from before me and even now numbers were vanishing beyond my own number of 41. People were vanishing everywhere and yet to the ones consuming others in one way or another it didn't seem to matter.

It mattered to me though. I don't know why, but it seemed like it should matter to someone at least.

"Is she always like this?"

Stonily, I remained standing, staring forward as yet one more man's hand ran over my body groping at whatever it wished to touch.

The other man in the room nodded and said, "Yes, she's something isn't she. Like a dumb time capsule or something of what it used to be like."

The man groping at my bare left breast let go only to slap me so hard that my head was thrown to the side. My face burning I straightened and with resolve I absorbed the pain as the two men laughed uproariously.

I turned my head back and for the first time I let my gaze fall upon the man who had hit me. I let my eyes reveal nothing but what I felt to be a cold disregard that I could only hope hid the anger that I felt inside.

If they knew they could make me angry it would be the death of me. These kind of demons fed off such human emotions the way people had once sat down to eat breakfast each morning.

My one and only defense was never to show emotion. My face was slapped to the side again and twice more the other way.

I said nothing in response to the abuse. They had paid my owners for the use of me and short of death I was at their complete disposal to use and abuse.

Strangely then they left me alone and I stood nakedly still as perverts that they were they began to kiss and make out with each other on the floor right before me. They didn't even know what to do with a woman anymore - now preferring instead the embrace of another man.

The thought of taking pleasure from the use of me seemingly no longer even occurred to them and for that I was truly grateful. Stoically I stood as in my presence an abomination occurred.

They were going to burn. We all were.

The only part of it that made no sense at all to me was why each night when I was released to go back to my cell the still small voice of the Creator that I'd given my heart to as a little girl still told me that I had value, that I was loved, and that He had a great and eventful future for me.

I didn't really believe Him anymore as that promised future got farther and farther away from being of any objectivity to me with each passing day I was forced to live through a daily hell.

Still, I didn't want His voice and calm assurances to leave, because then I really would go insane. At that point they would ship me off to worse pleasure dungeons than this one, where the survivors of Earth's many societal, economical, and natural disasters would pay every last coin to their name in order for a few moments of escape, even if it came at the cost of someone else's pain.

To them I was a slave and thus expendable. Sooner or later I'd break for good into little pieces and then there would be nothing left but for me to finally be sold off for the value of my meat.

The clock chimed and as the doors slid open behind me I turned from the two groaning men on the floor and left the room. Walking nakedly down the hall with my escort I was pushed into the cell that I shared with four other women.

Blessedly I slipped onto my cot and covered up with my blanket. I hated being naked.

I hated being cold too.

Ironically the only defense I had left to me was to be coldly indifferent and emotionally set-apart, only it seemed the longer that I was like that the more I became something different. Something without a true expression of purpose or point of self.

Gingerly, I felt at my face. It was sore, but thankfully not too badly swollen.

I'd gotten off easy tonight, but what about tomorrow?

Unfortunately, for a slave, tomorrow always had to come.

I was suddenly done with it all though!

There was nothing in it for me to keep surviving!

In the darkness of the cell I felt a tear course its way down my cheek as I recognized the reality of the moment. At last I was finally giving up.

At long last I was throwing in the towel.

The voice from within my spirit that nightly came to encourage me sounded out, "*Samira....*"

Holding a hand up in the darkness I whispered, "No. I'm done. I don't want You to leave me Lord, but I...... tomorrow I'm killing myself. I'd do it now, but I have nothing to do it with. I'm not changing my mind. I'm sorry to let You down after all this time, but I....I'm done. I... please ... don't talk to me. I...... I don't want to hear about love. I don't want any more hope! Please just let me die and let everything at last finally be quiet!"

Brokenly, I stopped whispering into the darkness. In the stillness of the room I heard nothing except for the breathing of others.

I heard absolutely nothing.

Crying I turned on my side and accepted the new reality that now I truly was alone.

There truly was nothing left to live for any more.

Lying there I waited in the darkness waiting to hear that voice of comfort speak but no voice came and in despair I stared at the wall before me.

I actually really didn't want to die, but now...... everything was over.

Without my God tomorrow really wasn't possible for me to handle anymore. Without really knowing the ramifications I had already killed myself.

Brokenly I whispered, "Oh God, I'm sorry! Please forgive me!"

With that moaned out revelation of internal misery expressed I suddenly found myself drifting into sleep and I went willingly into its comforting enclosure of numbness.

The End of Chapter One Excerpt

*The rest of the story can be purchased at Amazon.com and other online eBook retailers **OR** you could check in with me via email and if you agree to leave an honest review a free review eBook copy of the book may be emailed to you.*

The choice is yours – in any regard I deeply appreciate the effort to support me in my work; however, it is given.

Sincerely,

Aedan